DEMON SCOUT

DEMON SCOUT

CHARLEIGH FREDERICK

EBook ISBN: 979-8-88716-008-5

Trade Paperback ISBN: 979-8-88716-006-1

Hardcover ISBN: 979-8-88716-007-8

Cover design by Matt Guyor

Cover artwork by Matt Guyor

Published by Bow's Bookshelf, Inc.

Anna Stileski, Publisher

To my amazing parents, Chuck and Julie Frederick

PROLOGUE

Just past the Pits of Despair, but before the road to Hell, in the shadiest of neighborhoods, where the sun simply can't be bothered to go, and the only things that grow are demon children and mold, there is a small pub, its cabin-like exterior nearly covered in the thick web of moss lumping down from the roof. The door is always open, welcoming guests inside. For the few who can't fit through the door, large chairs line the walk up, filled with demons whose bodies spill over the edge like putty. Demons go there to dine and drink and talk about the misery they inflict upon you, your family, and the rest of the human race.

On this one particular night, the demon responsible for the Hundred Years' War filled mugs with the best mind-numbing drink, "Tears of Blind Rage," and slid them across the bar top to whomever could pay.

There was only one difference on this night. Toward the back of the bar was one rowdy demon who had no reason to be so proud of himself. Yet, he downed Tears like a victorious hero whose time was almost up. He laughed and talked to all who ventured his way, spending his savings on Tears for everyone.

"I'll tell you a tale of my last adventure, if you think it wouldn't shake you too bad!" he cried out with a laugh, each of his six hands jostling a drink, spilling them, and staining the plush red seat under his bum, the floor beneath him growing sticky.

Those sitting around let out a mighty cheer, egging him on, though he didn't need much egging.

"For those of you who don't know me, I am the demon Fawhikwuff and I have done the ultimate deed of terror! For I have gotten a child to burn his toys!"

Although it was the smallest of evil deeds committed by the demons in the pub, Fawhikwuff acted as if he had done something more vile than any of them. His attitude was infectious, though, so demons all around him raised their mugs and cheered and shouted anyway, praising a hard day's work.

The demons ranged in size and power. Some were the size of mice standing on their hind legs, others sitting outside were as large as the pub itself. Some glowed like a lit lantern, others seemed to be a vacuum for light, the space turning darker around them. Some could control minds, brew potions, and twist fates, whereas others could only make a child burn their toys. But despite their differences the demons held three things in common: They worked hard to commit deeds as evil as possible, for fear of being sent back to Hell. They lived and worked near the Pits of Despair or on Earth, not that any human would know. And they all knew Perlicudak, who had not yet graced them this evening with his terror, was the greatest and most powerful demon of them all.

In a corner booth in the back of this pub, surrounded by demons feeding off the freebies he handed out, was a demon who should have gone home hours ago when his friend left. "I am the greatest demon!" Fawhikwuff yelled, his drinks sloshing through the air once again, more landing down his front than entering his gullet. "Next round on me!" Every mouth in the bar cheered loudly.

Until the door opened, and in slithered a figure whose mere presence silenced the room.

Fawhikwuff didn't seem to notice as Perlicudak came in, a cruel look on his face as he scanned the crowd, as if looking for a face to challenge him.

"Come, my friends, and celebrate me!" Fawhikwuff called out. He may not have noticed Perlicudak, but he noticed the sudden fall in applause and merriment.

"Celebrate?!" Perlicudak slithered, the "sss" sound lasting longer than the rest of the word. "Why, I just love to celebrate. What is the occasion, demon?"

"I am the greatest demon, Fawhikwuff! Come, my friend, and drink with me!" Fawhikwuff cheered, still not realizing who he was talking to or noticing that everyone else had moved away from them.

"The greatest demon? I thought Perlicudak held such a title," Perlicudak teased, paying for a drink.

Fawhikwuff looked the greatest demon to ever exist straight in the eyes. "Perlicudak can go back to Hell and kiss Satan's butt. I'm the top dog, made in the shade. Tonight, my friend, I am the best, not Perlicudak. Now, come drink with us, friend!"

"And this 'us' is?" The humor had left Perlicudak's eyes as he looked around. The demons who had been celebrating Fawhikwuff moments before were fleeing. "Fawhikwuff, you common house fly, you are going to get hurt saying things like that. No one will ever fear your name as they fear mine. May your mouth be more careful in the future, before you get yourself into real trouble." Perlicudak was going to leave, was going to acknowledge Fawhikwuff's current state and act as if none of this had ever happened.

He was—until Fawhikwuff decided to keep talking.

"Now you listen here, my friend, I am the greatest demon

ever! I will rule a world one day! I am the amazing Fawhikwuff!"

"Would you say this to Perlicudak?" Perlicudak snarled, no longer in a good mood.

"Fawhikwuff has had too many Tears," the bartender interjected, trying to save his customer. But Perlicudak shushed him with a quick wave and a cross glance.

"Sure, I would say this to Perlicudak. Why not? Now cut the gas and come and drink with me!" Fawhikwuff swished his six mugs once more, splashing even more down his front.

"Fawhikwuff," the demon behind the bar warned, "watch your tongues."

"You watch yours," Perlicudak hissed at the barkeep before turning back to Fawhikwuff. "Fawhikwuff, how about a bet between you and Perlicudak then? Unless this is all just an act."

"Hey man, if Perlicudak wants to lose, that's fine with me."

"All right. We will swear it, and bind the bet on the River Styx in Hell so neither of us can back out then, shall we? If you cannot conquer one of the floating balls in our galaxy in the next human year, 365 human days, starting at midnight tonight and ending at the end of the human day on July 20th, 1969, then you will go back to Hell, never to hurt a soul on Earth again. You will die in Hell, as will your descendants."

"Oi! That's not fair!" the barkeep exclaimed. "You're trying to trick him. You barely know Fawhikwuff, and still you're making it a *human year*? That's not enough time and you know it, despite how long it sounds."

Perlicudak turned and hissed at the barkeep, whose mouth clamped shut, before he turned back to Fawhikwuff. "Do we have a deal, demon?"

Fawhikwuff nodded. "Okay, but when I win and take over a planet, this Perlicudak has to do the chicken dance here in the pub in front of everyone. He's going to be a chicken, and a duck, whether he wants to be or not. Cluck, cluck, cluck."

"You want Perlicudak, the most feared demon of all time, to do the chicken dance? That's all you want if you win? You don't want money or power?"

"He doesn't want to be a chicken. He doesn't want to be a duck. He can kiss my butt. Quack, quack, quack, quack," Fawhikwuff sang and stuck his tongues out at Perlicudak.

"Fine," Perlicudak hissed and moved directly in front of Fawhikwuff, holding out one of his tentacles. "On the River Styx we lock this bet. You're not getting out of this. And if you somehow manage to win, I, Perlicudak, will do the chicken dance here in the pub in front of everyone. When you fail to conquer anything, however, you will be spending the rest of your days in Hell. Agreed?"

"Agreed." Fawhikwuff set one of his six now empty mugs down on the table and reached out to shake Perlicudak's extended tentacle.

"Consider the deal set and locked. We both know perfectly well what happens to a demon who goes against a deal in the Styx."

PART I

NO ONE EVER LET ME MAKE A BET AGAIN!

1

364 DAYS, 17 HOURS, 12 MINUTES, 44 SECONDS, AND COUNTING TO CONQUER A PLANET

"W*ake up! Wake up! Wake up! Wake up!*"

Fawhikwuff rolled over in bed and slapped the side table next to it until the annoying chime shut off.

Begrudgingly, he sat up, his head pounding in pain.

"I shouldn't have been out so late," he muttered softly to himself. Lack of sleep always gave him a headache, and he knew that.

At least, he thought he had been out late. He didn't remember much of the previous night after his friend, Hesdihe, had gone home and another smaller demon with massive glasses had crowd surfed during karaoke. He had talked to a demon about selling toys, and the rest ... well, after that it was just a cloud of unknown.

Slowly, Fawhikwuff made his way into the only bathroom in his one-bed home. He flipped on the lights and winced, his eyes narrowing in protest at the sudden change. Today was going to be a long day; that, he already knew.

Looking at himself in the mirror, he was an ugly sight, even for a demon. Gently he ran four of his six hands over his face before he pulled the corners of his mouth open wide as to bare his teeth into the mirror. He had exactly four teeth—two on bottom, two on top—that filled his whole mouth. Even they looked tired and ready to go back to bed.

Fawhikwuff popped a couple of pain killers for his headache before he went back through his bedroom and to his closet. He had a few human suits in the back, as all good demons do, that he shoved aside to get to his work clothes. His employment required suits and ties, and, honestly, some days, Fawhikwuff would have preferred the human suits.

Fawhikwuff worked in the nightmare division to the left of the Pits of Despair. The company he worked for, Fright Nights, was the less successful of the two nightmare divisions, meaning he made less for the same amount of work. He didn't really mind, though. It was a justified salary: He did less work than his coworkers. His best friend worked by his side, authenticating names and creating nightmares, sending them out in order to torture whomever was next on the list. Satan would send the company names at the start of the week, and every day Fawhikwuff and Hesdihe ticked through those names, producing their nightmares.

They never got any high-profile people. Those went to the better division. People like Judy Garland, Audrey Hepburn, and Clint Eastwood would never be people for Fawhikwuff's nightmare-making skills. He was left to pain no-names, using failing tests, scary clowns, and missing pants: stuff like that.

It was honest work. At least that was what he told himself to get through the days. Truthfully, he hated his job, but it was the best of the options he had. It wasn't like he could make a living like the top demons did. Demons like Perlicudak went to the human world and possessed and tortured enemies of Satan for a living—people who most would describe as "good" and "kind" and "wouldn't-take-any-of-the-money-out-of-your-wallet-after-finding-it-on-the-street". They got to use every power they had on a daily basis, whether that be mind-control, or the ability to take all the oxygen out of the air. That was a real demon job, unlike making nightmares for people who didn't truly matter in the long run of the universe, or at least, didn't matter in the long-term of whatever the top demons had planned for the future of the universe. Whatever that was, Fawhikwuff knew it wasn't pleasant.

He finished getting dressed and grabbed an apple from the kitchen. Shoving the fruit into his mouth, he made his way quickly out the door and through his small, scorched-brown backyard, dodging his neighbor's pet giant scorpion. He got into his baby-blue 1950 Allard K1 car, its exterior smooth under his fingertips. His car wasn't old in demon years, but in human years, it was quickly approaching twenty. The demons may have been significantly more advanced when it came to technology, decades ahead of the humans, but the look of human cars, well, that was one area where the humans were superior.

Everything was looking like it was going to be a normal, crappy day of work for Fawhikwuff.

He parked the car in front of the office and made his way up to the front door. When he opened it, a wave of warm air hit him. So did a greeting from a demon he had met maybe once before. Louie? Loogie? He couldn't recall.

"Congrats! You're a brave demon!" *Oh, yeah, Lruquit. Like the sound a foghorn makes.* Lruquit greeted Fawhikwuff before walking past him.

"Um. Thanks?" Fawhikwuff answered politely. He climbed the grand glass staircase that led toward his office.

"Hey!" Valery from accounting stopped him about halfway up, a smile spreading across her emerald-green face. Fawhikwuff found it odd. She had barely ever even acknowledged his presence before. Her knife tail twisted around her like it had a mind of its own as she talked, her long tongue slithering out like a snake. "I heard about last night. That was kind of dangerous of you, wasn't it?"

Fawhikwuff nodded in confusion, his memories from the night before still a blur. Maybe she meant about his last trip to Earth? No one was ever that impressed with him for anything.

Valery's demon gift was that of persuasion. Although every demon could easily persuade a human, Valery was born with the gift so strong she could persuade anything and anyone. Fawhikwuff had heard she kept getting pests out of her house by simply asking them to leave. Apparently, the exterminators had been trying to recruit her for years.

"Yeah, a little dangerous, I guess." Fawhikwuff answered but had no idea what she, or Lruquit before her, was talking about.

"I like a creature that is in charge of a planet," Valery added.

"I mean, sure, who doesn't?"

"When you conquer one, save room for me," she hissed in his ear.

"Conquer one? Me?" He asked this mostly to himself, as she had already slipped by on her way down the glass stairs. She glided more than walked, leaving a trail of green slime.

Fawhikwuff picked up the pace heading up the stairs to his office.

The offices in his building faced either a small indoor courtyard or the great outdoors. As a lower-class worker, Fawhikwuff and Hesdihe's office had a window of the less-desirable outdoors. Nothing like staring at the Pits of Hell all day to put you in a bad mood.

He burst inside, surprising Hesdihe, who spun toward him, nearly spilling coffee out of his "Best Demon Ever" mug.

"Dude!" Fawhikwuff slung the office door shut and fell into his chair. "Valery just talked to me. Valery! From accounting! She has never talked to me before. Do I look good today or something? Because I don't feel like I do, but something must have changed."

"You don't look good. She probably figures either you'll be a huge success or you'll be gone." Hesdihe's machine was already on and Fawhikwuff could see he was working on a nightmare in which a guy's pants were pulled down and a beautiful red-haired girl was there laughing and pointing. Whoever this person was had truly angered Satan, and now Hesdihe was making the redhead laugh at him every night for a human month. He had gotten really good at the realness of her bouncing red locks.

"Hesdihe, what are you talking about?" Fawhikwuff asked, powering on his own nightmare machine, the screen glowing blue as the loading logo of a moon appeared. A cow jumped over the moon on repeat as the machine came to life.

"I'm talking about your bet with Perlicudak. It's all anyone is talking about."

"My what? What'd you say?"

"Hey, do you mind if I turn on the radio? They're doing a call-in giveaway for a really cool human suit."

"I don't care about the bloody radio, Hesdihe! What bet?"

"You made a bet with Perlicudak last night at the pub, like an idiot, after I left. This is why I told you to leave when I did. Guess you shouldn't have called me a party pooper, because at least I don't have a bet with the worst demon out there. Also, I lied about you not looking good. You actually look really awful. And you don't smell so hot, either."

Fawhikwuff looked blankly at his friend. "Why in the Pits of Despair would I take on a bet with Perlicudak? I don't have a death wish."

"You seriously don't remember any of it?"

"No!" Fawhikwuff grabbed the back of Hesdihe's chair and spun his friend around to face him. "This is worse than any nightmare you can create. What did I even bet? Please tell me it wasn't my comic book collection."

Hesdihe started laughing.

"It *was* my comics, wasn't it? This isn't funny, Hesdihe! I have some really cool ones!"

"No, sorry, your comic books are safe."

Fawhikwuff sighed with relief, leaned back in his chair, and ran two of his hands over his face. "Okay, so what is the damage?"

Hesdihe waited until he and Fawhikwuff were looking eye to eye, his five eyes blinking at his friend in harmony. "You, Mr. Fearsome Fawhikwuff, bet that you could conquer a planet."

"No."

"You bet you could conquer a planet within one year."

"Bloody no!"

"You bet you could conquer a planet within one human year."

"Bloody no!"

"If you fail, you have to go back to Hell."

"But it's dark and scary down there, and I don't like it!" Fawhikwuff argued.

"You swore on the River Styx."

Fawhikwuff ran another hand over his face. "Okay, so I can't back out then. But I also can't win. No way. Or can I? Maybe? I just need to find a planet, right, get to it, and conquer it in one human year." Fawhikwuff let out a guttural growl. "How could I be so stupid? Actually, don't answer that. Pubs are banned moving forward. For both of us. I'm sorry. They should be banned for everyone. I'm so stupid!"

"If you're waiting for me to argue with you, you're going to be waiting a long time."

"Are there any easy planets to conquer? I obviously can't conquer Earth. That's Satan's domain."

"He'll kill you and drag you to Hell himself before you lose the bet," Hesdihe agreed. "You want to know what the best part is?" He leaned a little closer.

"There's more?" Fawhikwuff moaned.

Hesdihe gave a small laugh. "All Perlicudak has to do if he loses is dance the chicken dance."

"That's it? I didn't ask for money or to be in the moving pictures with John Wayne or for him to go to Hell? Or anything? Of course, I didn't." Fawhikwuff took a deep breath. "It doesn't really matter what he has to do if he loses, though, does it? It doesn't matter. I'm not going to be able to conquer a planet. I am weak and dumb. I can only possess one person at a time and when I'm possessing someone, all I can do is be persuasive. I can talk people into things, but I can't make them give me a planet! How am I going to conquer a bloody planet?"

"Maybe don't shoot for a bloody one?"

"Har-har, Hesdihe!"

"Sorry." He chuckled at Fawhikwuff's distress. "How about you pick one that's empty?"

"And how, wise guy, do you think I'm going to get to an abandoned planet?"

"The humans are currently racing to get to the moon. I bet one of them will do it before the year is up. Just get close enough to one of the astronauts going on the trip and possess him. Help him get to the moon, kill the rest of them up there, where you won't have to clean up the mess, and claim the moon for your own. By what I heard, the moon would fit into the parameters of the bet - despite technically not being a planet."

"That's ... actually not a terrible idea. Would the moon count, though, to win the bet?"

"Sure, why not? I mean, it's not technically a planet, but it's like a planet, right? So, yeah, it'll count. And thank you, I am full of good ideas—like the radio." Hesdihe smiled and turned back to the laughing redhead, having the dream zoom in on her flawless face.

"I just find someone who is going to be an astronaut?" Fawhikwuff said slowly to himself. He was working the plan out in his head.

"Exactly!"

"Can you cover for me here at work?"

"You're going to be gone a whole human year. There's not a chance I will cover for you that long."

"Why not?" Fawhikwuff tried to make a pouty face, but it didn't really work with Hesdihe's back to him.

"Because I'm not doing the work of two demons just because you don't know how to keep your mouth shut at the pub. How many Tears did you have anyway?" Hesdihe didn't wait for an answer. "Go talk to Elvey. I bet if you ask nicely, he'll give you the time off."

"Yeah, right." Fawhikwuff stood, leaving the office on heavy, hurried steps.

He was in trouble.

Big trouble.

Part of him wondered if he should even try to win this bet or just keep working and enjoy what little time he had left before the River Styx forced him down to Hell. Either way, these next 365 human days were ones Fawhikwuff truly dreaded.

"Fawhikwuff! There's the demon we all love." A demon passing in the hallway, this one Fawhikwuff was certain he did not know, gave him finger guns as they passed. Fawhikwuff wanted to bury his head and hide.

Finally, he got to Elvey's office and entered without knocking. He was going to Hell in a year; what did it matter if he was a little rude to his boss?

"Fawhikwuff, I was wondering when I'd be getting your letter of resignation," Elvey greeted, his back to the door as he stood behind his desk facing his bookshelves, straightening the golfing trophies. It was a rather human sport, but Elvey loved it for some reason. He would even wear a human suit and compete in human golfing competitions in order to stack his shelves with the fake gold and little golfing figures. Fawhikwuff thought Elvey's time might be better used making the office he managed better, but to each their own.

"So, you heard, too." Fawhikwuff rubbed the back of his neck.

"That you had way too many Tears and made a stupid bet with Perlicudak and that now you have to find a way off our dirtball and onto another dirtball that will actually let a moron like you rule it? Fawhikwuff, it's all anyone can talk about right now. You really stirred the pit here, and you can't eat your way out of this stew." Elvey turned and sat down in his plush purple leather chair, his hands resting on his glass desktop. He stared Fawhikwuff down. "You're a moron, you know that?"

"Everyone keeps reminding me."

"Good. Not that it will help you up in the human world, but maybe you'll find a village who recently lost their idiot and you can fill in until you're sent to Hell." Elvey let out a deep sigh. "I care about you, kid, I really do. But you messed up here. Perlicudak has never lost a bet, so this is more a matter of pride for him than anything else. He won't let you win. He sent four good demons to Hell on bets last human year alone. *Good* demons. *Skilled* demons. You're more of a he's-got-a-great-personality-sorta demon. Perlicudak doesn't lose, so you better have a plan. A good plan. The flawless-est plan you're ever had. What is your plan?"

"I heard the humans are planning to go to the moon," Fawhikwuff started. "If I possess one of the astronauts, I can go up with them, kill the host, kill the other astronauts, and bing-bang-boom, Perlicudak is doing the chicken dance."

"How do you plan to get close to an astronaut?"

"I don't know that yet."

"How many people can you possess?"

"In one day, I can go possess and then exit a human once. Once in and once out, I mean. If I start the day in someone, though, then I can leave them and jump into someone new. It isn't recommended but it is possible. If you jump too many times without being you, if you possess too many people in a row, well then, it can lead to you being not you when you finally leave. Psychological damage and stuff. You know?"

"Yes, of course I know. I went to kindergarten, too, Fawhikwuff."

"Right, sorry."

Elvey gave a small nod. "Your possession game is weak."

"I know."

"How about oxygen?"

"How 'bout it?"

"Can you breathe without it? Or are you just a little more human than everyone thought?"

"No, I can breathe without it."

"Well, if you possess an astronaut, once you're in outer space, cut off the oxygen. The human astronauts will all suffocate and die. Then you say that somehow your oxygen is the only one still working. Ground control will still help you without catching on that you're a demon. I know I don't have to say it, but the humans cannot know that we demons are real."

"Elvey, you're brilliant."

Elvey gave a laugh. "You didn't think I got to be head of this company by my pretty face alone, did you?"

Fawhikwuff was tempted to tell the demon how unpretty his face was, but instead bit his tongue and said, "I guess not."

"Now, go clean out your desk, Fawhikwuff. I can't pay you when you'll be in Hell in a year, and I can't pay you when you're not here to work. If you do somehow manage to get to the moon and win, you are more than welcome to come back and work for us again. Sound good?"

"Yes. Thank you, sir."

He should have known better than to think he could get paid leave for a whole human year. It didn't matter much, though. He would be leaving his home and everything the currency he made here could be used to buy. Once he picked a human skin suit to assume, he would have to find a job there, with his new identity, in their awful human world, if he wanted to make any money. It was awful because he and his type tortured it, sure, but even still, he wasn't prepared to face it.

2

364 DAYS, 12 HOURS, 34 MINUTES, 08 SECONDS, AND COUNTING TO CONQUER A PLANET

Splayed out on Fawhikwuff's bed were three human suits —and one Fawhikwuff, who didn't know who to go to Earth as. All three identities were unique in their own way, and they all posed different challenges. He liked and hated all of them. No matter which one he picked, squeezing his entire demon form into the itty-bitty human form was never a fun task. Getting all six of his arms into the two human arms was a nightmare in and of itself.

Option one was named Gladius Haugen. She was older, so if he walked funny or said something odd, no one would notice. Her fingernails were Fawhikwuff's favorite part. They were long and painted red and made fun clicking sounds against hard surfaces. Gladius's hair, though, was a nightmare and a half. Earth dwellers expected so much of little old Gladius and her locks, and, frankly, Fawhikwuff wouldn't have the time up there to properly primp his — or, rather, her—hair every day if he wanted to get to the moon.

Option two was, as the humans would describe it, a greaser baddy bad boy. Fawhikwuff called him Jonny Style, which may have been a little over the top, but Fawhikwuff loved the persona. Jonny was on the edge and a total loose cannon. Fawhikwuff was all for that lifestyle. If he didn't act right, he could say "Well, doll face, that's just rock and roll," or something like that. He could figure it out along the way. In that skin he could get dirty, but just like with Gladius, he would have to style his hair every day for it to look like a Jonny Style signature style. Jonny also seemed to get arrested a lot, and Fawhikwuff really didn't have time for the human legal system.

Which left option three: a long, lanky, dark-haired, awkward-looking, middle-aged man named Chris Green. Perks with this one included wide, child-bearing hips that looked odd on a lanky man but gave him the ability to blend in pretty much anywhere. Down sides included those same hips and that he would have to get a boring job if he wanted to make money. No human was going to hire Chris to beat people up for not paying on time. Chris looked like the one who got beaten up. A lot. He was a man-child, which would be helpful. Fawhikwuff knew, if he ever needed to he could shrug his shoulders and say, "Jeez, officer law man sir, I'm just an American man like you. I don't know how that astronaut ended up in the trunk of my car." He knew from experience humans would buy that.

The choice was actually a pretty easy one. Fawhikwuff picked Chris Green up off the bed and gave a sigh of resignation. With a pained, hesitant look, he considered the dark mop of hair on Jonny's head.

A demon wearing a human suit was different from possession. With possession, a demon easily slides into the mind and body of a human. It's easy, quick, painless, and very draining. Putting on a human suit is none of those things, and it makes for a better disguise, as no one knows him or expects anything of him. Still, it was hard to shove a massive demon body into a small human suit. It was like cramming a bear into a prairie-dog hole.

Fawhikwuff accidently put the human suit on backwards

the first time and had to start over. But he figured it out, and he eventually got all his bits where they needed to be.

It may have been a struggle, but looking at himself in the mirror, he knew the feminine-waisted man was a good choice. He would be able to blend in. Perhaps he could look enough like a scientist to just waltz into NASA and wait around to possess an astronaut. Would they let him do that? He truly had no idea, but if anyone was stupid enough to open the front door and allow a demon inside, it was a dumb human.

3

362 DAYS, 12 HOURS, 49 MINUTES, 13 SECONDS, AND COUNTING TO CONQUER A PLANET

Fawhikwuff, in his Chris Green suit, began his long trek to the human world. He was confident he'd look like any human he met. He walked day and night, through the seven layers of deadly farts and through the sea of swirly-twirly broken hearts. Then he walked through a mind-numbing lecture and ended his journey somewhere in the state of Virginia, nearly two whole human days later.

"I need something to drink," he muttered, still tasting farts on his tongues as he looked around at the human world.

He would travel here now and then, but whenever he got here, it hit him like a ton of bricks why he preferred his office job in the demon world. He may have lived near the Pits of Despair, but the human world felt like a larger pit of despair and smelled even worse, was dirtier, and everyone just seemed so unhappy.

The worst part was, here, drinks didn't quench demon thirst.

His plan had seemed simple enough in his head. He was going to go to NASA, find an astronaut, and catch a ride to the moon like it was a taxi and he was a New Yorker. It seemed simple to him because he hadn't really thought it through. He would just waltz in. Assuming he could do that, how, without any help, would he figure out who an astronaut was and whether the astronaut was one of the ones actually going to the moon?

Okay, so it wasn't the greatest plan, but it was his plan.

Fawhikwuff looked up at the sky. The fireball was large and warm overhead. He had plenty of daylight and scorching heat ahead of him as he walked along the dusty sidewalk. Chris's dress shoes hurt his demon feet-stuffed-into-human feet, and as he walked, dust coated the shiny black shoe leather.

He was in an average-looking town. There was a general store, a liquor store, a church with a tall steeple that Fawhikwuff would avoid at all costs, a gas station with a sweaty man out front, and a large whites-only sign over the movie theater door. This was a town so encompassed by unnecessary hate that they would never notice a demon in their midst.

In his realm, demons came in all colors, so segregation was nearly impossible. Valery was a greenish-blue with an emerald tail. Hesdihe was a burnt orange like the sun in children's crayon doodles. Elvey was a shimmery silver with streaks of pastel pink. Perlicudak was neon blue. Fawhikwuff was a dark navy in color with swirls of purple and white. Someone had once called his color galaxy, but Fawhikwuff wasn't exactly sure how "galaxy" could be a color. Today, though, in his Chris Green suit, Fawhikwuff was a boring, one-toned white man — and that tone was pale.

He needed to ask someone where NASA was or, perhaps more pressing, where he could get a glass of water, and he couldn't seem suspicious.

He spotted a little table set up alongside a street with a girl behind it. He was in luck. Even if it wasn't a lemonade stand, kids gave out information without thinking twice. Quickly, he made his way over to the booth.

"Hello, mister. My name is Annie Mae, and I'm selling cookies for my scout troop. If I sell the most cookies in the country, then I get to—"

"Yeah, kid, if you don't have something to drink, I really don't care," Fawhikwuff cut her off. His eyes shifted to the spread in front of her and his mouth began to water. "Actually, what kinds are these? And do you hand out free samples?"

"We have chocolate mint, shortbread, chocolate coconut, chocolate peanut butter—"

"Coconut? From Tahiti? The Fiji Islands? Coral Sea?"

"Sure." The girl shrugged, unconvincingly. She started over. "My name is Annie Mae, and I'm selling cookies to win the grand prize, a chance to meet a—"

"Again, don't care. Is this seriously your sales pitch?" Fawhikwuff demanded, his nose turned up. "Come on, Annie, you can do better than that. Tell you what, you tell me where the NASA snobs are at, and I'll help you out, just this once. I can sell those cookies easy."

"You're going to buy a box of cookies?"

Fawhikwuff let out a laugh. "No! I don't have any money. I'm penniless. This skin didn't come with a wallet, unfortunately. I'll happily steal a box from you, though, after I help. Those coconut ones look like they'd be really nice after a drink or two. I have a weird taste in my mouth that I need to get out. Traveling to Virginia is not as easy as it sounds. Now, Little Miss Alleyway, or whatever, where can I find NASA?"

"It's by the pizza place, but it's all gated off. No one gets in." Annie Mae fiddled with the end of her braid as she spoke, her nails showing chipped remnants of pearl-pink nail polish. The unforgiving sun beat down on her pale skin, slowly turning it bright red.

"Alleyway-"

"It's Annie Mae, actually."

"Did you seriously just cut me off? I am a demon! It's my

high waist, isn't it? I should have picked Jonny Style. I bet you would show him some bloody respect. Chris just gets walked all over, even by children."

"You don't look like a demon."

"Yeah, well, you weren't supposed to know I am one. You don't look like a moron," Fawhikwuff snapped.

Annie Mae looked down at her table. "Chloe says I do."

"Well—" Fawhikwuff trailed off. He wasn't exactly the warm and fuzzy type, but he felt he couldn't just ignore a comment like that. "More humans than you think are actually demons in disguise, so, really, you should take what people—or, I guess, not people—say with a grain of salt, because they may be a demon. Chloe is probably just upset about something else and is manifesting her negativity all over you. You look fine to me. I guess. Though I don't really know the difference, so I'm probably not the best judge."

"Are you going to buy cookies?"

Fawhikwuff let out a breath he hadn't realized he was holding in, happy that the child was moving past the Chloe thing. "Annie Mae, you said NASA is by the pizza place?"

"Yeah."

"Okay. Does that mean that it's in this town?"

"Yeah. There's a base just outside town."

Fawhikwuff gave a whoop of joy and punched the air in a strange sort of celebratory dance.

"You look like an idiot," Annie Mae said with a giggle.

"I totally nailed it with directions!"

"My name is Annie Mae, and I'm selling cookies. If I sell the most cookies, I can win a chance to meet with-"

"Annie! Shut it with the speech, okay? Cut the gas. I get it. You have cookies. Now, which way is the pizza place?"

"I don't know."

"You don't know?"

Annie Mae shook her head.

"Annie, this is life and afterlife! Don't you drive? How do you not know where things are?"

"I'm twelve! I can't drive!" Annie Mae giggled again. "You're a funny demon. And I'm selling cookies for my troop. Would you like to buy a box? If I sell the most cookies in the country, I get to meet the man who will become-"

"Speech, Annie, zip it!" Fawhikwuff looked back down at the cookies and his Chris suit's eyebrows furrowed together. Gently, he picked up a box of the coconut chocolate cookies. "Annie Mae, why is NASA's logo on the box?"

"I'm selling cookie-"

"Cut to the good part, Annie, the clock is ticking here."

"NASA is sponsoring this year's cookie sales. If I sell the most cookies, then I win the chance to meet the man who will become the first to go to the moon!"

"Annie, are you for real or is this an elaborate prank? I swear if Hesdihe jumps out right now, I'm going to—wait, are you Hesdihe?"

"Huh?"

"Hesdihe, I'm going to be mad if that's you."

"I don't know what a Hesdihe is. Would you like to buy a box of cookies or not?"

"A box of cookies? That's what you're thinking about right now, Annie?"

"It's actually Annie Mae."

"You're going to meet an astronaut!" A real plan was forming in Fawhikwuff's mind now, and it was bringing a smile to his face. If he were to become Annie Mae, he could easily make the weak humans buy cookies from him. Then all he would have to do is waltz into NASA as little Annie Mae, cookie-selling champion of the world, and switch possession to whatever astronaut was going to the moon while she was meeting him. Then he would win the bet, so long as the humans made it to the moon within the next human year.

"I'm not going to win," Annie Mae said softly.

Fawhikwuff looked down at her with the face of Chris Green. "And why not?"

"I'll never sell more than Chloe."

"The girl who insulted your appearance? You know I could just kill her for you, save us both a headache."

Annie Mae shook her head. "No, don't kill her. It's just—Chloe is the most popular girl in school, and her parents are rich and buy all her cookies. She's already 'sold' so many." Annie Mae used finger quotes.

"Yeah, well, she's not a demon. Demons are better than rich parents."

"I'm not a demon either, though."

"Annie Mae, you're not a demon *yet*." Fawhikwuff cracked his neck and jogged in place a couple of steps. "Do you have a bag with you, Annie Mae?" He would need somewhere to stuff the Chris suit while he was Annie Mae.

"Yes. Why?"

"Great," Fawhikwuff said before he became Annie Mae, possessing her.

Her body was smaller and, under the blistering Virginia sun, warmer inside than the Chris Green suit. The first thing Fawhikwuff did was take off the sweaty vest and brown sweater the little girl had been wearing, before emptying her bag and shoving the Chris Green suit in. He zipped the bag shut before anyone could see. He would have to find someplace better to hide it, but for the time being out of sight would have to do.

"Hello, dear."

Fawhikwuff jumped and turned from the bag, pulling it behind his back. An older gentleman was at the table, looking at the boxes.

"How much for two boxes?" the man asked, straightening his bowtie and bowler hat. His face wore a friendly smile. It made Fawhikwuff's Annie Mae nose wrinkle.

"That's all you're buying, you cheap old fart?" Fawhikwuff demanded. All the man saw was little Annie Mae yelling at him. "It's fifty cents a box, you cheap old jerk. You're buying four boxes, give me two dollars," Fawhikwuff said with persuasion that he thought would have made Valery proud.

The man pulled his wallet out of the pocket of his mustard-colored vest, his eyes suddenly glazing over, like he was in a trance. Staring straight ahead, he handed Annie Mae the bills.

"You have a great day." Fawhikwuff handed the man the cookies and jammed the dollar bills into—he stopped. What he was wearing had no pockets. Why wouldn't there be any pockets? Where was Annie Mae keeping the money? And what sort of organization sends a kid out to sell things without giving their uniforms any pockets to jam money into for safekeeping? What sort of human noise was this?

Fawhikwuff jammed the bills into the bag alongside the Chris Green suit and muttered a few choice words under his breath before turning back to the table. Looking out at the empty street, he knew he wasn't going to rake in much money here, and losing wasn't going to be an option if he didn't want to go to Hell. He may not have known this Chloe girl or why she picked on Annie Mae, but he was fine killing her if that's what it took to win. He was going to be the top cookie-seller in the United States of America, and that was a demon's promise.

"Hells yeah," he said to himself, eyeing up a bar down the road. No one buys cookies like men in bars. That was a fact he knew from experience.

4

362 DAYS, 11 HOURS, 16 MINUTES, 48 SECONDS, AND COUNTING TO CONQUER A PLANET

"You will buy the entire case."

"I will buy the entire case."

"Good." Fawhikwuff smiled. He was enjoying how small his new form was and that his Mary Jane shoes were leaving delightful little footprints all over the polished bar top. His eyes locked with the bar's owner, whom he had just "convinced" to buy out his entire cookie stock.

If he had ever jumped on a bar in a pub in the demon realm, it probably would have broken, and he would have rightly been banned from the establishment.

"That will be six dollars." He finished off the transaction by spitting on the floor.

The bartender opened the till and pulled out the money, passing it to Fawhikwuff, who stacked the cash on top of Chris Green's head in Annie Mae's bag. One day and they had already sold out. He was going to be meeting an astronaut, and if selling cookies was the way to do that, then so be it. He would sell every cookie he could get his six hands on.

Now he just needed to find the source of the cookies so he could get more.

Fawhikwuff got off the bar and sat down on a red stool. All he had left was his bag and cash. Letting go of his control over the bartender, Fawhikwuff ordered a drink. He still had the taste of farts in his mouth, and it was hard to be in a good mood when all you could taste was farts.

The bartender looked at him with confused eyes as the haze cleared. "Annie Mae? What are you doing here? Do your parents know where you are?"

"I don't know." This was why demons wore human suits: It was better to be someone no one cared about. "I just want a drink, man."

The bartender opened his mouth as if to say something, before closing it and scanning the bar. His eyes landed on a man in the back, and his mouth opened once more. "Johnson! Can you drive Annie Mae home? Her folks are probably worried sick."

"Hey!" Fawhikwuff snapped. "I don't need a babysitter! I need a drink." If he was being honest, he wanted to be driven home so he could see where Annie Mae's house was. Then he would have somewhere to stay for the night. But he wasn't a fan of the bartender treating Annie Mae like a child, even if that was exactly what she was.

Johnson came forward, fanning open his jacket to show off his badge and gun as if he were an Old West character, ready for a quick draw. "Hey, Annie Mae, you remember me, right?"

"Sure," Fawhikwuff lied, though he doubted he would ever forget the guy.

"Good. How about you grab your stuff, and let's get you home?"

"All I've got is my bag." Fawhikwuff turned back to the bartender. "This isn't over," he threatened before grabbing the bag and waiting for the guy to show him out.

"What about your cookie boxes?" Officer Johnson, who Fawhikwuff noted had an abnormally large nose, asked.

"Bartender was nice enough to buy me out. Even if he won't serve me a drink, I suppose he's a pretty good guy. I mean what is his game in not serving me? Ageism? Is that still legal here?"

The bartender looked confused. "I did buy all the cookies. Why did I do that?"

"Oh, it's because I'm from Hell."

"Annie Mae, that's not a very nice thing to say about yourself," Officer Johnson argued.

Fawhikwuff looked away. If he wasn't careful, he'd blow his cover. Although he doubted these guys would believe him if he straight out told them he was a demon. "Just take me home, please, officer."

5

362 DAYS, 11 HOURS, 01 MINUTE, 43 SECONDS, AND COUNTING TO CONQUER A PLANET

"You know, Annie Mae, if there's anything you want to talk about, I'm here," Officer Johnson said with a kind smile as the two rode out of town.

"Yeah, I'm good, man. Thanks, though," Fawhikwuff said with a small head bob. He would go to Annie Mae's house, play nice, be this little-girl character, and, hopefully, it would lead him to more cookies to sell. He would win that contest; of that he was confident.

"Annie Mae," the officer tried again, "you seem out of it. What's on your mind?"

"I'm just thinking about selling cookies."

"Is that what this is about? Annie Mae, if it's getting you this worked up, perhaps you shouldn't be selling cookies. Meeting an astronaut isn't worth your health, after all."

"If I want to have a life in the future, it sure is."

"Annie Mae, they're just cookies."

"Maybe to you." Fawhikwuff nodded as the two rode up to a small home in the suburbs. It looked peaceful. "Is this me?"

"You don't recognize your own house? Maybe I should walk in with you and talk to your folks."

"No! Of course, I recognize my own house. Don't be ridiculous." Fawhikwuff desperately tried to remember the name to call the man, but he was blanking. "You, um, thanks for the ride." He opened the car door, grabbed the bag with Chris Green and the money in it, and bounded up the walk through a lush and meticulously manicured lawn toward a house just as well kept.

"Wrong house, Annie Mae!" Officer Johnson called from the squad.

Fawhikwuff stopped and turned back to the car. "Right. Wrong house. I am totally messing with you. I think the heat has gotten to my head; it's making me act goofy. You know how Virginia is." Fawhikwuff smiled at the man, waiting for him to respond.

The man simply stared back, clearly debating if he had to get out of his car.

"Which one then?" Fawhikwuff finally asked.

The man pointed left, and Fawhikwuff trudged across the perfectly green grass and into the scorched-brown yard of the house next door. Oh, yes, Annie Mae most certainly had the worst house on the block, and Fawhikwuff loved it with all twenty of his demon hearts.

The house's front door opened with a creak and a shutter. Inside, the place was dimly lit but the clutter and mess were unmistakable.

"Where do I get more cookies?" Fawhikwuff called out, slamming the door shut with a mighty bang. There were two closed doors to either side and a hallway ahead that led to a staircase. Whoever designed the house clearly liked the color plum.

A smaller, older woman emerged from one of the doorways on the left and stepped past a painting of a shipwreck that hung as crooked as a street-corner jewelry salesman. "Annie Mae, dear, how was the cookie-selling?"

"I sold out; now I need more. I have to beat whoever Chloe is and I have to win the contest. I have to be the top seller."

"Tone, dear."

"Uh-huh. How do I get more cookies, woman?"

The woman, taken aback, gasped quickly and, in an oh-my move, covered her heart with her hand. "Annie Mae, I don't like what this cookie-selling business is doing to you."

"My name is seriously Annie Mae?"

"I think so. I mean, that's what me and your father named you: Annie Mae."

"Barf."

"Excuse me?"

"You are excused. What is my last name?"

"What?"

"Last name. Go."

"Annie Mae, did you hit your head?" The woman came a little closer, her brows coming together as she studied who she thought was her daughter.

"No, woman, I didn't hit my head. I need to know my bloody last name! What is my last name?"

"Rumlered."

"Do you know, do the scouts have a demon category in the sell-cookies-win-a-prize business here?" Fawhikwuff would hate to go through all the trouble of dealing with Annie Mae if it was possible to do this on his own. There was something about the older woman that he guessed was Annie Mae's mom that felt off-putting.

"Where in the world did you hear about demons? Have you been going to church again? I told you, nothing good comes from that. You don't need it."

"I don't need church?"

"That's right."

"I mean, holy water sucks for me, so I'm going to have to

agree with you on that point, but what kind of Southern mom are you?"

"Just go wash up, Annie Mae, and make sure to keep your scout uniform out for the meeting tomorrow at the school. I don't need this today from you." The woman made a motion like catching a fly in midair, and she pinched her eyes shut.

"So which hole with a bed belongs to mwah?"

6

362 DAYS, 10 HOURS, 33 MINUTES, 41 SECONDS, AND COUNTING TO CONQUER A PLANET

"This Hong Kong flu seems to actually be getting serious," Annie Mae's father muttered, mostly to himself.

"I wish you wouldn't read that paper at the dinner table, Walter," Annie Mae's mother scolded as she poured a cup of coffee for the graying man holding his newspaper. Fawhikwuff could only see the top of the man's head poking out from the top of the page. A large bold headline on Fawhikwuff's side screamed something about taxes. Or maybe zoning. The demon couldn't care less.

"Would you relax, Helen? It's not in the states. Not yet at least," the voice behind the paper muttered.

Annie Mae's mother made a tsking sound as she went to the oven and pulled out what looked like a giant hunk of meat in a pan. "What else is in there, Richard?"

Fawhikwuff's ears snapped to attention. He could have sworn the woman had just called the man Walter. Why was she now calling him Richard?

"Nothing exciting, dear. New Jersey and New England governors want to control how the whole nation handles guns,

Jonny Beach is making news, and there's a fine-China sale going on downtown this week. Weren't you looking for new plates? Or was that Billy's wife?"

Fawhikwuff was shocked the man hadn't noticed his wife calling him different names. Fawhikwuff had written nightmares like that for guys who thought their wives might be cheating on them. Walter and Richard weren't even similar names.

"Here you go, Annie Mae," the woman said as she set a plate with a hunk of the larger hunk of meat that had just come from the oven and a dollop of white potatoes down in front of him.

"Thank you." He was excited to not have to cook for himself for the foreseeable future, even if it was just gross human food. Someday perhaps, the humans might flavor their food as well as the demons.

"Henry, dear," the woman turned to the man, "your darling Annie Mae was driven home today in a squad car by Officer Johnson."

Henry now, too? It's her husband. She should know his name. How do you not know your husband's name?

Henry or Walter or Richard or whatever his name was folded his newspaper and set it down next to his plate on the table. "Officer Johnson? That man is an arrogant di-"

"Darling!" the woman interjected.

"Right, right." The man put his hand in what little hair he had left. "That's still not a very sweet thing for such a sweet girl to be doing. Getting driven home by cops. What will the neighbors think? Did something happen to you when you were out selling cookies?"

"I sold out," Fawhikwuff said, feeling like that was the only thing of note for the girl to recall—not that she had jumped on a bar, met a bartender with a conscience, or, oh yeah, gotten possessed by a demon. Though, he was the demon, so why would he mention that?

"Sold out? Of cookies?"

"No, morals. Yes, of course, cookies," Fawhikwuff snapped at the man.

"That's wonderful! Isn't that wonderful news, Penelope?"

"Just wonderful." The woman nodded her head as she set a plate of food down in front of the man.

Penelope? Was this just their thing? Calling each other random names? Fawhikwuff was flabbergasted. What even were their real names?

"I suppose a ride from Officer Johnson isn't the worst thing. It's not like you were arrested or anything," the man said as he slid the newspaper out from under his plate and, with a dramatic flurry, snapped it back open, once more hiding his face.

"It's not bad at all," Fawhikwuff chimed in. "He was just being nice. I'm fine."

Annie Mae's mother sat down with her plate of food, and the man gently folded his paper, setting it down and signaling the start of dinner by picking up his fork. "Thank you, Mary," he said with a smile to his wife, whose cheeks reddened slightly, and a smile spread across her face.

"Anything for you, Nelson, dear," she said softly.

This house was weirder than Fawhikwuff could have imagined. If awkward family dinners weren't a demon invention, the humans really ripped themselves off.

Tomorrow he could go to this Annie Mae's scout meeting and get more cookies to sell. The game was afoot, and this was one demon who came ready to win.

7

361 DAYS, 13 HOURS, 21 MINUTES, 34 SECONDS, AND COUNTING TO CONQUER A PLANET

School.

Not just any school.

Middle school.

Not even actually school yet.

This was scouts, which, really, was just a group of awful preteen girls with less supervision than in real school because they were trusted to be responsible—a fatal error made by the public school system.

Fawhikwuff had gone through Annie Mae's belongings the night before and had learned that Annie Mae was in the sixth grade in Ms. Bratwurst's class. No, Bratwurst wasn't the teacher's real last name, but it was close, and Bratwurst sounded way cooler right now to Fawhikwuff's growling stomachs. Though, any food that wasn't what Annie Mae's mother cooked would be fine by him. The breakfast of runny glop—oatmeal, yeah, right—had been worse than the meat plate the night before. Ms. Bratwurst was also the scout leader, meaning, he presumed, he'd be seeing a lot of her.

Fawhikwuff made his way through the courtyard in front of the school. Little pink flowers smiled up at him in the morning sunlight. It was nothing like the decrepit schools he put in people's nightmares. This was good research for his job, if nothing else. The more believable things are, the scarier they can be. A pleasant courtyard in front of your beloved school and then "BAM!" Your greatest fear hits you.

He didn't think he would, but he was missing his job. He hated it when he was there, but he missed talking with Hesdihe and creating something to be somewhat proud of everyday.

"Well, if it isn't Miss Stupid, stopping to smell the flowers."

Fawhikwuff turned and saw a girl as small as Annie Mae glaring at him.

"Me?" he asked in surprise. Was he seriously getting bullied by a child? He was a demon! Of course, as he had to remind himself, he didn't look like a demon at the moment. He looked like Annie Mae, who this girl probably knew. Still, he had half a mind to end her then and there.

"Of course, Miss Stupid." The blonde girl took a step closer, a whiff of perfume accompanying her, her two friends staying back and snickering. "Who else would I be talking to?"

"Yourself?" Fawhikwuff suggested.

"No one likes you, Annie Mae," the girl sneered.

"Sorry, who are you again? I only remember *pretty* faces."

One of the blonde girl's friends gave a loud snort. The blonde girl flashed her a glare before turning back to Fawhikwuff. "What's in the bag? Clean diapers?"

"Why? Do you need one?" Fawhikwuff crossed his arms, still not totally used to having only two instead of six. He had Chris Green and the cash from cookie-selling in the bag. He had been worried Annie Mae's mother might find Chris Green if he left the bag at the house, and he couldn't risk that.

"Slap yourself," Fawhikwuff ordered, persuasion in his voice.

The blonde girl slapped herself, hard. "What was that?" she demanded in shock.

"You must be Chloe, right?" Fawhikwuff couldn't help but grin.

The girl nodded sheepishly as she stared at her hand like it was a boy who had betrayed her trust, terrified that she would hit herself again.

"I suggest you get out of my face from now on, Chloe. I am the only queen here." Fawhikwuff walked away from the girls and made his way to the door. He hated bullies.

8

361 DAYS, 13 HOURS, 00 MINUTES, 48 SECONDS, AND COUNTING TO CONQUER A PLANET

Fawhikwuff settled into the back of the classroom in an uncomfortable wooden chair. He was glad he was in Annie Mae's small frame; anything larger and the desk would have burst, popping him out like a zit. He wondered if humans ever thought like that? Did they ever wonder, if they were to go out and just eat pies until they weighed a thousand pounds, whether they could be popped like zits? Humans seemed fragile enough. This was an idea he wished he had had when he was working on making nightmares. He had to get this idea to Hesdihe, whether he lost the bet or not. How unpleasant a dream would that be? To just have two large sausage fingers pop you? It was brilliant!

"Good morning, troops!" A stout woman greeted the room as she entered. A chorus of "Good Morning, Miss" followed from everyone but Fawhikwuff. "Welcome back, ladies." The troop leader was old, ugly, and had hair so tall Fawhikwuff guessed she had to duck when going through doorways. How did that towering nest not make her stout frame top heavy? Fawhikwuff couldn't help but marvel.

He saw that Annie Mae was one of eight girls in the troop.

He saw Chloe and her two friends, another girl who looked nice but so far hadn't said anything to anyone, a girl who looked way too young to be there and who had her thumb in her mouth, a larger-set girl with her feet defiantly up on the desk in front of her, and a girl who had made a headband out of a strip of toilet paper.

Fawhikwuff was liking his chances.

"All right, if you have sold any cookies please come up and bring me the money so we can get you counted toward the total," the scout leader instructed as she picked up her clipboard and smiled warmly at the group of girls.

Fawhikwuff opened Annie Mae's bag only as far as necessary to reach around the Chris Green suit and pull out the wad of bills, his prize for selling out. Quickly, he zipped Chris Green back inside and stood up to get in line behind Chloe and her minions.

"How many did you sell?" Fawhikwuff tapped Chloe on the shoulder, hoping she hadn't sold out, too.

"Was that the wind I heard?" Chloe mocked, and her friends snickered.

"I don't know. Did you fart? You sure smell like you did. Seeing as you're large enough to be a tree, though, I can see why you would think the wind would be talking to you. That or maybe you're going mad. Sorry, I was trying to make small talk, but seeing as you're such a-"

"Good job, Lilith!" The scout leader's praise cut off Fawhikwuff. "Sold out again this week."

Fawhikwuff knew the true Lilith, the mother of demons, and he was grateful to see the girl looked nothing like her. That would be the last thing he needed. "She sold out?" Fawhikwuff demanded in a hushed tone.

"Her dad is selling them at his office," one of Chloe's friends whispered back before receiving a stern glance from Chloe.

"That's cheating," Fawhikwuff sneered, as if using his demon abilities to peddle the product wasn't.

"No, it's not." Chloe turned on Fawhikwuff, her arms crossed and her glare stern. "It's called using your resources, Miss Stupid."

"So, your parents are hustling your goods, too." Fawhikwuff nodded at the realization. Annie Mae was lucky he had come, as her parents wouldn't sell them. Their parents were why these girls were doing so well. He needed to cut off their worker bees or else he was going to have to work twice as hard, which he didn't want to do.

"And how are you selling?" Chloe asked as the girl with toilet paper for a headband gave over her money to the scout leader. It only looked like a few quarters. Good.

Fawhikwuff was selling through manipulation and demon persuasion. "The normal ways."

He glanced back to Annie Mae's bag and thought about the Chris Green suit. If he was a grown man, he could get a job and sell cookies at his workplace. Or he could find where his fellow scout mates' parents worked and get jobs and then get the parents fired.

Man, that sounded like a ton of work. Fawhikwuff shook his head. He wasn't going to do all that.

"Some people would say having a parent help them is normal. You know, people with parents who actually love them," Chloe sneered. "London, you go ahead of me," she said to one of her minions. She moved to be directly in front of Fawhikwuff. She stood backward in line in order to face him. "Annie Mae, you will not beat me. You won't beat anyone here or elsewhere in the country. I will be meeting the astronaut who is going to walk on the moon and there is nothing you can do about it, because you are weak and dumb." She had a wicked smile on her face, one that said she was better than everyone else.

"Boop," Fawhikwuff responded, bopping the top of Chloe's nose with one of Annie Mae's fingertips.

Chloe looked like she had just been pantsed or, rather, skirted. That was a look Fawhikwuff knew pretty well, thanks to the nightmare division.

"You are such a—"

"Chloe, it's your turn!" the scout leader called, cutting off the insult Chloe was ready to hurl.

Chloe turned away from Fawhikwuff and went up to the woman. "Here. I sold out. Again."

"Very good, Chloe! That makes two girls who have sold out today!" the leader said as she took the money. "Same amount this time?"

"Oh, yes, and trust me, I will sell out again." Chloe looked back at Fawhikwuff, baring her teeth like an animal before a fight. "And again. And again."

"I'm sure you will, Chloe," the troop leader said with a smile as she handed Chloe a case of cookies.

Chloe glared at Fawhikwuff as she made her way back to her desk.

"Annie Mae, dear, it's your turn." The scout leader smiled.

Fawhikwuff moved forward and smacked down the wad of bills on the woman's clipboard. "I sold out, too."

"Annie Mae, that is extremely impressive! I am so proud of you!" the scout leader said, beaming.

"What do you mean?"

"I'm proud of you. It means I'm happy because you have achieved a great feat." The scout leader slowed down her pace as she talked.

"I'm confused."

"I'm so sorry, achieved is kind of a big word."

"What? Do you think I'm two years old?"

"No, Annie Mae, you're twelve."

Fawhikwuff shook his head, not understanding what was

happening. "I know what achievement means. I know what proud means, too. I'm not a baby. I'm confused why you're treating me differently. You didn't act like this when Chloe or Lilith sold out. You're acting like—like there's something wrong with me."

"Well, dear, Chloe and Lilith are ... normal."

"So, if Toilet Paper Head over there sold out, would you react like this?"

"Well, no, Lolli is normal, too."

"Her name is the first half of the word lollipop and she wears toilet paper as an accessory. Are we sure normal is the right word? I think I should be deemed more normal than someone wiping their butt with the same thing they're putting in their hair."

"Maybe we should discuss this later," the scout teacher said softly, looking rather uncomfortable.

"No," Fawhikwuff pressed. "Why are you patronizing me?"

"Annie Mae, you were born different. Special. You know that."

"Isn't everyone born different? Isn't that kind of the point of you people?" Fawhikwuff asked. "Like, even identical twins are born different."

"You're a little bit slow, Annie Mae, that's all."

"Okay, old lady. That's uncalled for. Foot race. Right now! Me versus you. We'll see who's the slow one, you bag of jelly. Your hair will tip you over in the first few feet."

"That's not what I mean." The troop leader set her clipboard down on her desk.

"Then what do you mean?"

"Birdbrain!" Chloe yelled from her seat and started making bird sounds. The rest of the troop began to snicker at Annie Mae, and Fawhikwuff felt her cheeks warming and reddening.

"Chloe," the scout leader scolded before turning back to

Fawhikwuff. "You just struggle a little with reading and social cues. It's nothing to be ashamed of."

"I want triple."

"What?"

Fawhikwuff looked up and locked eyes with the woman. "This birdbrain is going to sell more than everyone else here. I want triple. I'm going to prove to all of you that Annie Mae has got this. I'm going to beat all of you. Just because she needs a little more help—I mean, just because *I* need a little more help —doesn't mean that I won't run cookie-selling laps around all the jerks in this room. Now give me triple."

9

361 DAYS, 04 HOURS, 12 MINUTES, AND 46 SECONDS, TO CONQUER A PLANET

"I'm home!" Fawhikwuff yelled as he entered the house belonging to Annie Mae. He had already sold an entire case of cookies to a store owner on his way home, and now he had only two cases left with him.

He had an inkling now why everyone acted so strangely toward Annie Mae, and if that was how they wanted to play things, he would use it to his advantage. He would destroy them. Annie Mae may have a few roadblocks in her life, but that meant nothing in the grand scheme of things. Everyone is different, after all. No two paths are the same.

And Annie Mae now had the advantage of a demon watching out for her.

Annie Mae would soon be the top cookie seller in the United States of America, meet an astronaut who would walk on the moon, and help Fawhikwuff not to have to go to Hell.

Fawhikwuff smiled and headed up the stairs at the end of the plum-painted hallway, a newfound confidence filling him.

10

327 DAYS, 14 HOURS, 22 MINUTES, AND 08 SECONDS, TO CONQUER A PLANET

Selling cookies and proving everyone wrong was going great. Fawhikwuff soon left Chloe in the dust in total sales. He was confident he'd win, but he knew he had to keep up the pace. Chloe proved to be a daily problem, but Fawhikwuff found ways to shut her up. Really, her mean-girl trash-talking was no match.

As the cookies sold, he picked up more boxes at the scout meetings, which were held twice a week until school started in the last week of August. On the first day of actual school, Ms. Bratwurst started the way annoying humans always do, with roll call.

"Harold Anderson?"

"Here."

Why did she read off names as if they were questions? It wasn't like people didn't know what this was. She says your name and either you answer or you're dead to the class. It was an easy concept to grasp.

"Fern Appleton?"

"Here," said one of Chloe's minions.

Is that just what being a human was like? You spent a tenth of your life just saying where you were? Who cared if someone was missing? Either they'll show up or it's their loss.

"Ty Bernstein?"

"Present."

Oh, and of course there's always that one kid who insists on spicing up the answer. You're not cool for doing it, you're just annoying because the whole thing loses its pace and takes longer to get through.

"Ursula Biroc?"

"Yep."

Ugh. Cue the gag sound. Just when you thought "present" was a terrible answer, they hit you with a "yep," as if that's even an answer to "say if you're here when I call your name." Humans are truly terrible.

"Finn Davidson?"

"Here."

Finally, a good person.

"Eve Duckworth?"

"Here."

Now we're starting to get moving again. As long as no one else decided to get wise, Fawhikwuff saw green flags and smooth sailing ahead.

"Lilith Fehl?"

"Present."

Grrr.

"London Galiano?"

"Here," said Chloe's other minion.

"Chris Hamilton?"

"Here."

"Chloe Kennedy?"

A silence fell over the room, and the teacher's head snapped upright to scan her pupils, searching for Chloe.

Fawhikwuff knew why Chloe wasn't here. He had made her run off crying before the bell. It had been glorious, better even than when he had made that child burn his toys before this whole mess had started. Chloe had kept going on about Finn to her friends, and Fawhikwuff had used some elegant language to explain why the sweet boy, Finn, would never be interested in someone like Chloe.

Day one of school and he was already improving life for his host. What a great parasite he was. When he gave Annie Mae control back, her life was going to be far more splendid and, hopefully, a little easier.

"Chloe?" Ms. Bratwurst asked again. "Has anyone seen Chloe?"

London raised her hand. "Annie Mae made her cry. I think Chloe went to the nurse's office to compose herself."

All heads spun toward Fawhikwuff. "Okay, first off, in case anyone missed it, London is a snitch. Second, Chloe had it coming. She was bullying me first. She said a guy would never like me. I stood up for myself and said a similar thing back." Fawhikwuff looked at London. There were a lot of things he wanted to say to her, to call her, but he couldn't get Annie Mae into that much trouble, so he just went with a simple, "Meanie."

"Annie Mae, we do not use that sort of language to refer to our friends," Ms. Bratwurst scolded.

"Well, in that case, it's a really good thing London is not my friend."

"Oh, go to Hell!" London spat back.

"London!" Ms. Bratwurst exclaimed.

Fawhikwuff gave a humorless laugh. If only London knew the irony of what she had just said. "Where do you think I came from, darling?"

"Annie Mae, principal's office," Ms. Bratwurst ordered with a finger pointed to the door.

Fawhikwuff stood and grabbed his bag with Chris Green still stuffed safely inside before heading out the door with one final salute to the troops. Now he just had to figure out where the principal's office was.

11

327 DAYS, 04 HOURS, 18 MINUTES, 42 SECONDS, AND COUNTING TO CONQUER A PLANET

"No daughter of mine will be saying such ghastly things!" Annie Mae's mother exclaimed as she loaded up plates with food, making a lot of noise as she did, further showing how upset she was at Annie Mae. "William, perhaps you have something to add?"

William now?

Annie Mae's father looked up from his newspaper. "Ah, shucks, Polly. I just got home. I don't want to deal with this right now."

"And you think I do?" Annie Mae's mother placed plates of food in front of Fawhikwuff and Annie Mae's father.

"It's your job, Molly, not mine."

"Really, Owen, you need to help out more."

The father stood, tucking his newspaper under his arm and picking up his plate. "I'm going to go and eat in the den away from all of this."

He left, and the mother dropped into her chair, sobbing.

Fawhikwuff didn't care the man left. He turned his focus to the slop humans called food. Demon food was so much better.

"Look at what you did, Annie Mae," the woman accused

through her tears, as if this was somehow his fault. He wasn't a marriage counselor.

"He's your husband, lady. I didn't make you marry him."

"You upset James, and now he left. If this keeps happening, one of these times he may leave further away than the den."

"Again, that's a real *you* problem. Also, what even are your guys' names?"

"Is that all you care about? Is this what you want, Annie Mae? You want your father to leave us?"

"You can both leave for all I care." Fawhikwuff shoveled food into his mouth.

"You are an abomination!" Annie Mae's mother left, too, still crying, giving Fawhikwuff a bit of peace to go with his "meal."

Annie Mae had aced her Latin test earlier, not that anyone cared, he thought.

12

326 DAYS, 12 HOURS, 51 MINUTES, 43 SECONDS, AND COUNTING TO CONQUER A PLANET

"Hello?" Fawhikwuff called out as the brass bell over the door chimed, signaling his entrance into the shop and alerting the old man behind the counter. "Would you like to buy some cookies?"

"Shouldn't you be in school?" the man barked.

His shop was on the smaller side, and although the sign out front labeled it as an antique store, it looked more like a used bookstore with your grandma's furniture resting every few feet, just to spice it up.

"Shouldn't you be six feet under?" Fawhikwuff snapped back as he placed the case of cookies on the man's counter.

"I don't remember stocking these." The old man picked up the case and straightened his glasses to examine it. "How much did the sticker say it was?"

"I'm not buying these, Grandpa, you are."

"I am?"

"You will be," Fawhikwuff said with a deep sigh.

. . .

"Here you go," the man said, his eyes glazed over as he handed the money to the little girl, who gently slid off the man's counter, money in fist, before stuffing the bills into the Chris Green suit's mouth. He had made the man buy both cases and now he was yet again sold out. The scout leader would be eating her words at their next meeting.

No one would call Annie Mae a birdbrain again, not after she won.

Fawhikwuff couldn't wait.

13

326 DAYS, 10 HOURS, 21 MINUTES, 37 SECONDS, AND COUNTING TO CONQUER A PLANET

"Le latin est ma confiture, femme," Fawhikwuff said, leaning forward in the small desk.

"Annie Mae, that is enough. I don't approve of such language in my classroom," Ms. Bratwurst scolded.

"You challenged me, woman!" Fawhikwuff defended.

"I did not challenge anyone. Now, class, please open your books to page 216." Ms. Bratwurst went back to the front of the classroom and leaned against her desk, a teacher's version of the textbook open next to her.

Fawhikwuff opened up Annie Mae's bag, shoved Chris Green's face aside, and pulled out his Latin book. He didn't need it but figured he'd follow along anyway. As a young demonling he had learned this all in his school, which had been far cleaner and held more passion for learning than the dank halls of the United States public educational system. Not that he was complaining. He knew he had gotten himself into this mess. Now he was Annie Mae, the underdog, as he liked to think of her.

"Does anyone remember how to count from one to ten in Latin?" Ms. Bratwurst asked.

Fawhikwuff's hand flew into the air. This was the most basic and rudimentary Latin he had seen since preschool.

"Annie Mae? You remember?"

"Nullum excrementum, Sherlock."

"Excuse me?"

"Sorry, got something caught in my throat there. One through ten. Unus, duo, tres, quattuor, quinque, sex, septem, octo, novem, decem."

"Very good, Annie Mae! So impressive."

"Stop doing that," Fawhikwuff ordered.

"Stop doing what?"

"Patronizing me like I'm a dumb child. I know Latin. I am fluent in Latin."

Ms. Bratwurst shook her head. "I am not doing that."

"You are! You don't even know Latin. I do. I could teach this class."

Ms. Bratwurst scoffed, a little more loudly than she intended, which only confirmed Fawhikwuff's suspicions. "Of course I know Latin. I am teaching it."

"Non ducor duco. What does that mean then?" Fawhikwuff did challenge this time.

"I will not stand for such anarchy in my classroom!"

"Oh, my gosh, she doesn't know," London loudly whispered to Fern. The entire class, who also had no idea what Fawhikwuff had said in Latin, began to snicker.

Ms. Bratwurst's face was turning red. "It means ... it means ... I lead not by duty."

"Ha! She said duty!" One of the boys in the back began laughing.

All eyes went to Fawhikwuff to see if the teacher was right. Fawhikwuff loved all the power he had just gained and didn't want to give it up. "Oooh, so close. But no, that's not correct. Acta deos numquam mortalia fallunt." Fawhikwuff looked around at the kids in class. They were all so excited and supportive of his questioning of the teacher. He felt like he had just risen an army of the dead, which he hadn't done for about a century now. It was intoxicating and pushed him to keep needling his patronizing human of a teacher.

"Annie Mae, it's time to settle down," Ms. Bratwurst ordered.

"I should teach the Latin class. You know, it might help to have someone in charge who knows the language. You treat me like a child, but darling, you're a fraud, and that's so much worse."

"Annie Mae, leave my classroom—NOW!" Ms. Bratwurst growled.

"Worth it." Fawhikwuff grabbed his bag and shouldered it, saluting the class on his way out the door. Cheers erupted from the students, but other than that, they did nothing to challenge his being thrown out. Not that he minded. He had two cases of cookies to con humans into buying.

14

324 DAYS, 13 HOURS, 19 MINUTES, 07 SECONDS, AND COUNTING TO CONQUER A PLANET

"C." Chloe spoke with confidence, although she really shouldn't have.

"Actually," Fawhikwuff said, raising his hand into the air, not waiting to be called on, "the answer is B. The book clearly states that the mitochondria is the powerhouse of the cell on page 198. Anyone who actually did the required reading would know that." Fawhikwuff gave Chloe a smug look. The girl glared back at him.

"Very good, Annie Mae! That is correct. Chloe, good try, dear," Ms. Bratwurst nodded with a smile.

"Teacher's pet," Chloe grumbled under her breath.

"Teacher, I think Chloe has something more to say," Fawhikwuff said with a grin, knowing full well what Chloe had just said would get her into trouble of some sort.

"Excellent! Chloe, please share," Ms. Bratwurst looked so excited, Fawhikwuff almost felt bad for her. It was clear the woman wanted an intellectual conversation, but all she was going to get was petty little-girl fighting.

"I, uh—" Chloe looked around the room. Every eye was on her. "Uh," she said again as her face began to turn red.

"That's okay, Chloe, we can just move on." The teacher nodded and turned back to the chalkboard where she was recording the answers.

"No," Chloe said. "I do have something to say."

The teacher turned back to her. "Well, go ahead then."

"I think it's strange that a birdbrain," Chloe turned an icy glare at Annie Mae, "is getting any answers right, don't you?"

"Chloe, that's not a nice way to talk about yourself," Fawhikwuff said, and the class erupted into laughter. "You're not that big of a birdbrain."

"I'm talking about you!" Chloe snapped. "It's like you're a completely new person, and it's not fair! Something happened to you, Annie Mae, and I swear I will figure it out."

"Well, that's a pretty big promise from a birdbrain who didn't even know the answer to a simple science question."

15

322 DAYS, 09 HOURS, 21 MINUTES, 37 SECONDS, AND COUNTING TO CONQUER A PLANET

"Ladies, I have exciting news!" Ms. Bratwurst said as she hurried into the room at the next troop meeting. "Our troop has been offered a place in the Hickey Hill Scout Camp this weekend! There will be a lot of chances to earn new badges and even more chances for group bonding!"

"A camp? Like in the woods again?" London asked.

"Cabins in the woods, yes, like last year. Same camp." Ms. Bratwurst nodded.

"Is there indoor plumbing this year?" Fern asked.

"Well, no. But there are very nice outhouses."

"Ew," Chloe said.

"Don't worry, Chloe." Fawhikwuff turned to look at her. "You don't have to come. You wouldn't be missed, and then there are more badges for the rest of us. Not that you would win any anyway."

"Oh, I'm coming, Annie Mae," Chloe growled back and turned to Ms. Bratwurst. "Put me down as coming.

"Well, I love your enthusiasm, but everyone who wants to come on the trip has to get a parent to sign this form and bring it back to me Wednesday." Ms. Bratwurst began passing papers around to the girls.

Fawhikwuff looked at his. He couldn't remember the last time he needed a parent's permission to go somewhere. Annie Mae's parents really didn't seem to care where she went, so leaving shouldn't be an issue, but he had never needed them to sign anything before.

"What if our parents don't sign?" Toilet Paper Head Girl asked.

"Then you can't come on the trip."

"But what if we really want to come?"

"Forge it and lie," Fawhikwuff called out, and the girls, except for Chloe, all gave a small chuckle. They were going to go and spend a weekend in the woods. How exciting.

Fawhikwuff didn't understand camping or why the humans enjoyed it. All these girls had homes with indoor plumbing, proper heat, good beds, and their own things, yet humans chose instead to go live in worse conditions and call it a vacation.

"Chloe's just nervous about the boys' troop across the lake," the plus-sized troop member with her feet on thè desk said. All the girls were getting more comfortable with calling Chloe out ever since Fawhikwuff had started pulling the crown down off her head.

"I am not!" Chloe argued.

"Didn't you date one of the troop boys, Chloe?" Toilet Paper Head Girl asked with a snicker.

"Adam probably won't even be there."

"Ooh, Adam. Sounds out of your league, huh?" Fawhikwuff asked.

"For your information, Annie Mae," Chloe glared, "since it's clear you are too dumb to remember, I broke it off with Adam."

"Yes, because you caught him kissing another girl," Fern said.

"All right, ladies, that is enough," Ms. Bratwurst said as she picked up her clipboard once more. "As for cookie sales, our current top seller is Ms. Annie Mae." Ms. Bratwurst gave a small clap that the other girls half-heartedly joined. "And I have sent in our current cookie-selling numbers. In a week or two, the head office will be sending back the figures for all the troops in the contest. Hopefully, a few of you will be on the list of current top sellers."

"I better be," Fawhikwuff muttered to himself as he stuffed the permission slip into his bag, accidentally punching Chris Green in the eye.

16

317 DAYS, 17 HOURS, 47 MINUTES, 59 SECONDS, AND COUNTING TO CONQUER A PLANET

"Twenty-eight bottles of coke on the wall! Twenty-eight bottles of coke! Take one down, pass it around, twenty-seven bottles of coke on the wall!"

Fawhikwuff truly hated the song the girls were singing at the top of their lungs as the bus bounced along toward camp, but man, did he love to watch how much Ms. Bratwurst and the bus driver hated it.

To put things in perspective, the girls had started with three hundred bottles of coke on the wall and had been singing during the entire trip, with the girl who wore toilet paper being the evil mastermind behind it. Perhaps, Fawhikwuff thought, she wasn't as bad as the rest of them.

The path to the cabins was rather beautiful. Fawhikwuff didn't mind a change of scenery to get his mind off the list that was coming soon. It would tell him if he was close at all to succeeding in his plan to sell the most cookies, or if he had been wasting a lot of time and needed to jump ship and find a different way to get to an astronaut. He couldn't just roll over and go to Hell. He wasn't ready for the heat.

"Twenty-four bottles of coke on the wall!"

17

317 DAYS, 16 HOURS, 02 MINUTES, 19 SECONDS, AND COUNTING TO CONQUER A PLANET

"Welcome to Hickey Hill Scout Camp, ladies!"

All the girls sat on the floor in a cabin Fawhikwuff assumed would become the mess hall. Their troop leaders were standing in the back, and all the girls from the troops were sitting on the floor in the middle of the room, making Fawhikwuff feel a bit like a caged animal.

There must have been six different troops represented. The lady who appeared to be in charge stood in front of them in an army-green dress that didn't look appropriate for the woods. A little too "formal wear". And she had a large smile on her face that seemed painted-on as thick as her eye shadow.

"This weekend we have invited you troops here because, according to our data, you are the troops which have collectively sold the most cookies nationwide! Our current top three sellers to this point are in this room, and if they keep selling as they have, well then, I think it will be one of the girls in this room who will have the honor of meeting a future moonwalker."

The girls began talking amongst themselves, filling the hall with an excited buzz. One particularly loud girl exclaimed, "This is so exciting!"

Fawhikwuff looked behind him and saw a troop that looked like someone had made ten clones of the same basic pretty blonde girl. He turned back to the front. If he were to just kill all the girls here, he would be winning for sure. Of course, then Annie Mae would go to jail and his plan would be completely foiled. She didn't have the muster to pull off mass homicide, unfortunately.

"On Sunday afternoon before you all leave, we'll be posting the current cookie rankings for all the girls here! During your weekend, we hope you'll be able to relax and learn many new valuable skills. If you participate in all the courses, you can earn up to six new badges! Now, we are going to dismiss you by troop. Your troop leader will be in charge of leading you back to your assigned cabins. You'll have half an hour to settle into your rooms. Then, we'll all meet back here for dinner. Saturday is going to be a long day, so after dinner, you'll be expected to go to bed. Tomorrow night, though, we will have a bonfire after dinner! Now, troop forty-two, from Frederick, Maryland, you are free to go!"

A uniform group of girls, all with their hair up in French braids, got up and left.

"Troop eighty-nine from Churchill, Virginia, you are free to go!"

The blonde clones from behind Fawhikwuff got up and sauntered out.

Fawhikwuff rolled his eyes and, while looking up, noticed a spider in the rafters of the wooden cabin. Its web was between two beams. Spiders were often demon children's pets, and he couldn't help but smile at the small creature.

Soon, Fawhikwuff's troop was called, and after the other girls stood up around him, he left with them for the cabin.

18

317 DAYS, 15 HOURS, 28 MINUTES, 56 SECONDS, AND COUNTING TO CONQUER A PLANET

"Annie Mae is a bed-wetter, so she should be on the bottom bunk," Chloe taunted as the girls entered their cabin. Ms. Bratwurst stayed outside, meaning Fawhikwuff was on his own in the den of dragons, with Chloe breathing fire at him.

"I am not a bed-wetter, Chloe," Fawhikwuff protested. Granted, he didn't mind a lower bunk. He wasn't fond of heights; it's a demon thing. But he wasn't about to let brown-nosing Chloe win at anything. As long as he was in control of Annie Mae, no one would put her down. No one would beat her. Ever.

"Annie Mae, you wet the bed last year. That makes you the bed-wetter!" Chloe crossed her arms, a triumphant look on her face, thinking she had just won. Oh, what a fool she was.

"Maybe, Chloe, I was just curious what it was like to pee on a bully, and I decided to test it out on you in the middle of the night. If you want, we can try out the experiment again, or you can just step aside." Fawhikwuff shoved past Choe and tossed the bag with the Chris Green suit in it up on a top bunk before getting up there himself.

"I am not a bully," Chloe argued.

"Finn would disagree." Fawhikwuff pulled out the name of Chloe's current crush with ease. The look he got in response made it clear this was war. Well, Chloe, bring it on. "We had a lovely chat the other day about it, just the two of us." Fawhikwuff had won many a war. This one would be the easiest. "Anyone else want to challenge me?" Fawhikwuff called out and was met with silence.

19

317 DAYS, 15 HOURS, 02 MINUTES, 19 SECONDS, AND COUNTING TO CONQUER A PLANET

Dinner wasn't great: baked beans and some sort of slimy sausage that wasn't exactly warm. But it was better than Annie Mae's mother's cooking, so Fawhikwuff considered himself well off.

He was the first from his troop to sit down, which allowed him to take in the room. It wasn't long before he realized the troops were all sitting together.

Chloe changed that. She went and sat on the other end of the room from Annie Mae, and the rest of the troop followed her.

Not that it bothered Fawhikwuff. Demons didn't care what groups of human girls thought of them. He didn't care that he was eating alone.

"Hey."

Fawhikwuff looked up from his runny bean mix and saw Toilet Paper Head Girl standing in front of him, her tray in hand.

"Hey," Fawhikwuff greeted back. "Everyone else is over there." He gestured to where Chloe was smiling at London, who was yammering on about something, probably nail polish.

"Is this seat taken?" Toilet Paper Head asked, gesturing to the chair across from Fawhikwuff.

"No, please, sit." A small smile played on his lips.

20

317 DAYS, 13 HOURS, 32 MINUTES, 08 SECONDS, AND COUNTING TO CONQUER A PLANET

The second Fawhikwuff entered the cabin after dinner, he felt the shift in temperature. The girls all turned a cold look in his direction.

"What's going on?" Fawhikwuff asked softly, freezing in the doorway.

"How about you tell us?" Chloe's voice cut through the crowd that parted to reveal her standing in the middle of the cabin, holding up the Chris Green suit. The runny beans dropped in Fawhikwuff's stomach. Like an idiot, he had left his bag in the cabin during dinner. It would have been so easy to just bring it with him.

With her nastiest look, Chloe asked, "What is this? It looks like a skinned person. Just wait until we tell everyone. You'll be thrown out for sure."

This had been a bad idea.

Fawhikwuff was so sick of this place.

He couldn't do anything right.

"It's nothing," he said, feeling as weak as he thought Annie Mae was. If he showed his true form, well, then, they would fear him. No one would dare touch his things and everyone would come and sit and eat with him instead of stupid Chloe. Not that that had bothered him.

"Did you kill someone?" Chloe asked. "They're going to throw you out for this, Annie Mae. This will be the end of your cookie sales."

No.

This wasn't fair for Annie Mae.

A burning guilt filled Fawhikwuff's gut. It wasn't Annie Mae's fault that he hadn't been careful enough. It wasn't her fault that Chloe found the Chris Green suit.

Fawhikwuff raised both hands into the air and closed his eyes. He had no choice. "Tempusquisusin!" he yelled. When he opened his eyes again, everyone in the room was frozen like a picture.

Fawhikwuff left Annie Mae's form and turned toward her, seeing her as frozen in place as the other girls. A hateful glare at Chloe played on Annie Mae's face.

He had to move quickly if he wanted to make it out without being caught.

Fawhikwuff ripped the Chris Green suit from Chloe's smug hand and forced his way into the thing, becoming a middle-aged man in a girls' cabin. It would be just as bad to be caught in here in the suit as in his demon skin, but at least this wouldn't reveal demons to the human world. Being the man would also help him not be caught on his journey back home.

He ignored the part of him that said not to go as he managed his six hands into the suit.

Once he was in the suit, he went girl by girl and gently removed the last fifteen minutes from their memories by pressing his fingers to the girls' foreheads, the memories raising out of their brains and into his hands. He hoped taking the last fifteen minutes would be enough. Some demons could take more than the last fifteen minutes, but Fawhikwuff was only fifteen minutes powerful.

He wondered how many people had met a demon and simply had their memories wiped so they couldn't remember.

Fawhikwuff reached Annie Mae last and stopped.

He had already taken so much from her; he couldn't bear the thought of taking her memories, too.

Silently, he slipped into the night, unfreezing the girls with a wave of his hand, careful not to free their memories, and leaving only Annie Mae to remember any of what happened.

21

314 DAYS, 12 HOURS, 02 MINUTES, 34 SECONDS, AND COUNTING TO CONQUER A PLANET

Back in his boss' office, Fawhikwuff couldn't help but notice that the fake gold golfers staring down at him from the trophies on the bookcase bore the same judgy, skeptical expression as the demon facing him from the other side of his desk.

"So, you're back?" Elvey finally spoke.

Fawhikwuff only nodded, resisting the temptation to point out the obvious, that they wouldn't be having this conversation had he not been "back".

"It's only been like a week. Are you seriously giving up?"

Fawhikwuff tilted his head. "I'm not giving up. I'm giving in. Everyone here knows I never had a prayer of winning that bet. That's why Perlicudak made it with me in the first place. I can't win. I never could. The sooner I embrace that the better for everyone."

"You don't think you can win?" Elvey leaned back in his chair. "So, what now? You come back and work a job you don't really like because, after a lousy week, you decide you just can't hack it? Fawhikwuff, you have over three-hundred human days left. Is this really how you want to spend them? Just waiting to be sent to Hell?"

"What should I do then, Elvey?" Fawhikwuff shifted in his chair, relieved to have all six of his hands back out in the open so he could sit comfortably again.

"Not give up for once in your life. Fawhikwuff, how long have I known you? Your dad worked for me. I remember when you would run around this place as a little demon, and you were as much of a quitter at age three as you are now. If your dad was still with us, he would tell you the same thing. Finding a way to the moon shouldn't be that hard for you. The humans are literally in a space race. They send crap up there all the time. So why not you? This shouldn't be so hard."

Fawhikwuff looked past Elvey at his golf trophies. All the judgment weighed on him. "Because you know the human race so well, right?"

"Better than you, apparently."

"You're not giving me my job back, are you?"

"I'm doing you a favor, Fawhikwuff. Someday, you will thank me for not letting you give up on this. Now, get back to Earth and send Perlicudak to Hell."

"Actually, if I win, he doesn't go to Hell," Fawhikwuff replied, sheepishly.

Elvey furrowed his gemstone eyebrows. "What does he have to do if you win then?"

"The chicken dance."

"That's it? Fawhikwuff! Jeez, man!"

22

314 DAYS, 11 HOURS, 56 MINUTES, 12 SECONDS, AND COUNTING TO CONQUER A PLANET

"Well, aren't you a sight for sore eyes." Hesdihe smiled when Fawhikwuff stuck his head into his old office.

"Elvey won't give me my job back," Fawhikwuff explained, "so I'm just popping in. I'm not staying."

"Elvey also won't hire anyone to replace you. He's planning to hire you back; you just have to win this bet first."

Fawhikwuff gave a loud snort.

Hesdihe paused the nightmare he was working on. The image on the screen showed an old mansion slowly exploding, trapping the helpless human's entire family. Truly a masterpiece, and Hesdihe was setting it aside to talk to Fawhikwuff. That made Fawhikwuff smile.

"So, what's your plan?"

"I don't have a plan. I'll probably just go back home and watch human trash on the box." Fawhikwuff rubbed his temple.

"That's stupid."

"Not you, too. I just explained this to Elvey. It's not giving up if you never had a shot."

"It is very much still giving up," Hesdihe argued. "You're not being smart, Fawhikwuff."

"Making it as one of those human things is harder than it looks, Hesdihe, okay? They are all so complex. I got thrown into a world where a twelve-year-old was calling the shots. She's a child. I got thrown into being this 'Annie Mae', who got dealt a really bad hand. Her parents clearly don't care about her, yet blame her for everything, including their bad marriage. She has no friends, which is actually helpful for me for blending in. But it is terrible for her. Everyone underestimates her and treats her like she isn't smart, and there's another child who seems to have made it her personal mission to hurt Annie Mae with words any chance she gets. You have no idea what human life really is. Honestly, Hesdihe, I really doubt you ever will, because you are comfortable down here. You have no drive to take a risk. At least I'm doing something."

"Yeah, you're going to Hell. Really inspiring right there."

23

314 DAYS, 01 HOUR, 57 MINUTES, 43 SECONDS, AND COUNTING TO CONQUER A PLANET

"You giving up then?"

"Well, they don't exactly take demons in the scouts, now, do they? And there's no other way to go see an astronaut."

"What if you went to their house? Or to NASA?" the barkeep asked as he dried a glass with a pure white rag.

"No, there's no other way," Fawhikwuff grumped, dismissing the two very good ways the drinks-serving demon had just laid out, and just off the top of his head.

"It's a shame the only paths to the humans are ones on Earth. Wouldn't it be nice if there was a path right to the moon?" the barkeep said with a laugh.

Fawhikwuff nodded. That would be nice. Though if there was a path that easy to the moon, another demon would have already claimed it. "The only way is to become a scout and sell the most cookies and beat Chloe and then, be introduced to an astronaut. Then I can catch a ride to the moon. That is my plan. That is the only plan."

"Except that plan failed."

"Exactly why I'm here."

The door to the pub opened with a bang, and wouldn't you know it, it was Perlicudak strutting in, a triumphant look on his face. He instantly spotted Fawhikwuff sitting at the bar and strolled over, sitting down next to his fellow demon with a grin. His face reminded Fawhikwuff of the one Chloe made every time she caused someone else to feel bad.

"You know," Perlicudak started, "when they said you had given up already, I assumed they were joking. This bet has barely even started. Why would you have given up? Don't get me wrong, though, I'm not disappointed or surprised in the least."

"Why are you here, Perlicudak?" Fawhikwuff asked, twirling a wooden stir stick in his drink.

"I had to see for myself. I had to see the piece of trash the tide brought in. I knew you were a loser and a quitter when we made the bet, but this? This is just pathetic. It's been one human week, lad."

"I knew it wasn't going anywhere."

"Well, I hope you enjoy your time left here, because, mighty soon, your year will be up and then it's back to Hell with you."

"Are you done gloating yet?"

"Are you done losing yet?" Perlicudak's smile grew, showing off three rows of hundreds of razor-sharp teeth. "Guess not."

"Perlicudak, I get it, okay? Really funny stuff. You can go now."

"You couldn't hide yourself from children. Human children found you out. What kind of demon are you? Some time in Hell may do you some real good. You can learn what a real demon looks like. I guess I'm doing you a favor in a way. You should thank me."

Fawhikwuff looked down at one of his hands as he began to feel an odd tingling.

"I deserve a thank you!" Perlicudak continued laughing,

taunting, and teasing, sounding to Fawhikwuff like a vacuum cleaner grabbing something it shouldn't.

Fawhikwuff ignored him as he watched his hand and then his arm and then the rest of his body begin to glow like a cracked glow stick.

Perlicudak noticed the light, too, and stopped teasing, his smile faltering for the first time since he had come in. "What is happening to you, Fawhikwuff?"

"I think I'm being summoned!" Fawhikwuff replied in surprise. Most demons weren't summoned anymore, not since they had found their own paths to the human world. But, of course, spells and rhymes were still out there if one knew where to look for them and had a specific demon in mind.

"Who in their right mind would summon you?" Perlicudak demanded, a jealous glare in his eyes, confirming Fawhikwuff's suspicion that he was indeed being summoned. "Clearly they must not know that you are such a failure."

"I have no idea who would summon me," Fawhikwuff assured, glowing even brighter now, filling the entire pub with a blinding glare.

"Maybe it's the kid?" the barkeep suggested.

"Annie Mae?" Fawhikwuff shook his head. "No, that can't be it. What would she want to see me for? I messed up her life enough already."

"Who else would it be?" The barkeep seemed to be the only one unconcerned that Fawhikwuff was beginning to resemble the sun and was being summoned. Other customers were fleeing the pub.

Fawhikwuff's vision began to blur, overcome by the blinding white. "I guess I'm not done yet," he muttered before the world around him faded away.

As he came to elsewhere, colors appeared in his vision one by one, like he was part of a strange paint by number that was being finished. He pinched his eyes shut, and when he opened them again, he saw he was in Annie Mae's bedroom. Standing before him, both with towels tied around their necks like capes, were Annie Mae and the girl who wore toilet paper headbands.

"It was you!" Fawhikwuff cried out as Annie Mae blew out the candle she was holding. She wore a pot on her head like a hat and a smile on her lips like it was a holiday.

"You're back!" Annie Mae cheered.

24

313 DAYS, 23 HOURS, 48 MINUTES, 03 SECONDS, AND COUNTING TO CONQUER A PLANET

"Okay, let me get this straight," Fawhikwuff said with a small smile. "You two scouts decided to summon me, a known demon who had been possessing you, Annie Mae, because you want me to continue to school Chloe? Really? You guys thought it would be easier and smarter to summon a literal demon than just come up with your own comebacks and burns and put-downs to handle a school bully? You thought this was smart?"

"Yeah," Annie Mae said, still smiling.

"That's about right." Toilet Paper Headband Girl shrugged, as if summoning a demon was just something one did to take care of a bully.

"Okay." Fawhikwuff rubbed his temple. "Where are you two on the leaderboard for cookie sales?"

"I'm not on the board," Toilet Paper Headband Girl said. "I've only sold three boxes."

"Three boxes? Not cases? That's it?"

"Yeah, boxes. My dad was snacky one night and ate three boxes, thinking my mom had bought them from the store. He had to pay for them, and he was not happy."

"Okay, Annie Mae, where are you on the board?"

"I'm number two." Annie Mae held up two fingers.

"Number two?" Fawhikwuff pinched his eyes shut. "Annie Mae, I have been selling my butt off to win this. Who has more cookie sales than you? And how?"

"Her name is Courtney Karen Clauson," Toilet Paper Headband Girl said. "She's from Churchill, Virginia, just outside of Washington, D.C."

"Okay, good. Now we just need a street address, and we'll go kill her. Get her out of the competition, and then Annie Mae is number one."

"No!" Annie Mae exclaimed. "We need to win the right way."

"Eh." Fawhikwuff wrinkled his large, oblong, already-pretty-wrinkled nose. "I'm not really in the business of doing things the right way. Or the legal way. Or what's socially acceptable, in case you haven't noticed. I *am* a demon."

"We do this right," Annie Mae repeated, crossing her arms.

"Well then, I don't see how me, a demon, is going to be much help to you, a little, pretty-much-helpless human girl."

"What are you talking about?" Toilet Paper Headband Girl demanded. "You were the top cookie-seller when you were Annie Mae. Well, you almost were. It was close between you and Courtney, like two cases close, and you weren't killing people back then."

"You weren't, right?" Annie Mae asked.

"No, I wasn't, but I was using my demon powers to make people buy the cookies, which, last I checked, is also very morally wrong and considered cheating. I, however, don't care if I am cheating, because, right now, the most important thing to me is meeting that astronaut."

"Why?"

"So, I can possess him and get to the moon. I need to conquer the moon, or another one of the floating balls in our galaxy, by the end of the human year, or else I'm being sent back to Hell. And trust me, not even a demon wants to be down in that hole. It's nasty and so hot. Like honestly, would it kill them to get an air conditioner or something? Even a fan. They're already dead, so the answer is no, it would not."

"Yeah, that checks out." Toilet Paper Headband Girl nodded. "I say we go with your original plan and con everyone into buying cookies. But I'm with Annie Mae. We don't kill anyone."

"What about maiming a few people? If we have to? You okay with that?"

"No."

"Brutally torturing?"

"No!"

"A little friendly dismemberment?"

"No! How can that be friendly?"

"Is mental and psychological warfare off the table?"

"Aren't those the same things? You know what, doesn't matter. All of this is no, no way, big old nada." Toilet Paper Headband Girl held out the last word for so long that by the end it was just ahhh.

"You ankle-biters are no fun," Fawhikwuff grumbled. "I ask for only one more thing."

"What?" Annie Mae asked.

"I need an answer. What's with the toilet paper headband?"

"You don't like it?" Toilet Paper Headband Girl touched the flimsy paper barely holding onto her hair. "It's an act of rebellion. It goes against conforming with society's image of beauty and wealth."

"I literally don't know your name, ankle-biter. In my head, I've just been calling you Toilet Paper Headband Girl. If no one knowing your name is not the goal, I'd lose the butt napkins."

The girl crossed her arms and rolled her eyes. Before she could reply, Annie Mae chimed in: "We have another problem.

Thanks to you, my grades are really low. It's like you weren't even trying."

"I wasn't trying. What does it matter?"

"It matters," Toilet Paper Headband Girl said, "because if Annie Mae's grades slip below a C average, she can't be in the scouts, meaning, no more selling cookies, meaning no trip to meet your astronaut, meaning no matter how many cookies you manage to sell you go to Hell."

Fawhikwuff pinched his eyes shut. "Great. We're going to lose."

"No!" Toilet Paper Headband Girl passed him a textbook from the floor. "You just have math homework to help Annie Mae with, seeing as you were the one in class."

PART II

LITTLE GIRLS ARE THE REAL DEMONS

25

FALL INTO WINTER

He was going to be the top cookie seller in the United States of America, and that was a demon's promise. He banded together with Annie Mae, and Toilet Paper Headband Girl, whose name, it turned out, was Lolli, kind of like the first half of the word lollipop. Although Fawhikwuff didn't venture back into the classroom, he and Lolli helped catch Annie Mae up on what she had missed, and with the three of them working together, they kept her grades afloat. In the afternoons, Fawhikwuff, as Annie Mae, ventured into the world and sold out of cookies faster than the girls could replace them with full cases.

As September chilled into October, Annie Mae's grades were solid Bs, and Fawhikwuff was confident in their chances of being top cookie sellers. The day before Halloween, the troop leader shared the most recent cookie-sales numbers, and, sure enough, Annie Mae had pulled ahead of the girl from Churchill. Lolli and most of the other girls were thrilled for Annie Mae, but Fawhikwuff was told Chloe had started calling Annie Mae names like birdbrain and pillock, so on the night of Halloween, Fawhikwuff made Chloe's witch costume more trick than treat. He made it so Chloe couldn't wash off her green face paint, and, worse, a real mole formed where she had applied a fake one.

Lolli thought it was hilarious, but Annie Mae was not amused. She was the most mature of the three. She made Fawhikwuff promise to change Chloe back, and the two settled on January 1st as the day Chloe would go back to her awful-looking self.

On November 5th, Richard Nixon won the presidential election. Annie Mae's father seemed pleased by it, but Fawhikwuff could sense a demon had a hand in the victory.

The U.S. launched Pioneer 9 to see if it was safe for man to go to the moon. Fawhikwuff eagerly awaited the all-clear. When Apollo 8 was announced, Fawhikwuff was elated.

Soon, jack-o'-lanterns turned into turkeys and turkeys into twinkling Christmas lights. On December 20th, a surprisingly big snowstorm hit Virginia with winds and drifts that made travel impossible—including for school buses. Normally, like all children, Lolli and Annie Mae would have no issue with schools-closed snow days, but when those days ran into Christmas break, well, that was a problem. There was no way to get more cookies to sell.

26

212 DAYS, 13 HOURS, 40 MINUTES, 33 SECONDS, AND COUNTING TO CONQUER A PLANET

"Tell me again why I can't just go steal some cookies for us to go out and sell? I'm great in the snow," Fawhikwuff said from where he sat on the floor, wrapped in three blankets. Annie Mae was pacing back and forth in front of him, and Lolli, who was covered in enough snow to make a small snowman, sat dripping all over Annie Mae's bed.

"Because, if the cookies get stolen, we can't very well go in and hand in the money and say we sold them," Lolli growled with a shiver. "I'm moving to Florida when I grow up."

"Okay, so what then? We just chill through winter break here and wait to lose?"

"The competition doesn't end until June 7th. We can stand to get a little chilled this break. Honestly, it will be kind of a nice break. Annie Mae, what's the status of your homework?"

Annie Mae stopped pacing and turned to look at Lolli. "I'm all done. I'm actually all done." She sounded a little surprised. "All through break."

"Already?"

"Yes." Annie Mae nodded her head. "I'm all done!" She

returned to her pacing back and forth, wearing a groove into the once-plush carpet.

"Good. I wish I was done." Lolli nodded and then readjusted her toilet-paper ribbon. "The last thing we need is for you to lose on account of grades."

"She's good, woman. Give it a rest," Fawhikwuff said.

"We have to win," Lolli retorted.

"And we will. And if we don't, there's always Plan B." Fawhikwuff grinned an evil grin, evil even for a demon.

Lolli sighed. "Plan B is killing the real winner, isn't it?" she asked.

"No killing!" Annie Mae insisted again.

27

212 DAYS, 12 HOURS, 59 MINUTES, 54 SECONDS, AND COUNTING TO CONQUER A PLANET

"Honey." The knock came at the bedroom door again. Fawhikwuff was trying his best to find a place to hide in case Annie Mae's mother decided to just let herself in. Annie Mae was no help, continuing to pace even as Fawhikwuff eyed up Annie Mae's bed, noting that it was about the same size as he was and wondering if he could fit under it without getting stuck.

"I saw your friend leave." Her mother's voice struggled to come through the door. "It's almost time for dinner. May I come in?"

"No!" Annie Mae said and abruptly stopped pacing long enough to glance, even if only briefly, at the demon in her room. She resumed her steps, back and forth, back and forth.

"Your father would like to see you," her mother called again with another little knock. "Are you okay? Did your friend upset you?"

Annie Mae shook her head and then remembered her mother wouldn't be able to see her through the closed door. If she could, there would be a whole other issue. "No," she called out finally.

"Oh, let her be, Jane!" Her father's voice carried up the stairs from the kitchen below. "More pot roast for us. If she wants to live like a shut-in, I say we let her."

"Just a moment, Rodger!" mother called down the stairs.

"Come on, Nancy!" father bellowed.

"I said just a moment, Richard!" Mother's voice was louder this time, as if she was facing the door again. "Annie Mae, I'll scoop a plate for you. Come down when you're hungry, and it'll be waiting."

Fawhikwuff and Annie Mae could hear her mother's feet rattle down the stairs, back to the plum-colored hallway and through the main part of the house. Her husband, whose name Fawhikwuff still did not know, waited for her so he could fill his gullet with whatever she placed in front of him.

"What are your parents' names?" Fawhikwuff asked quietly.

Annie Mae stopped pacing and looked at the demon, now sitting on the edge of her bed, crushing the mattress under his weight. "Betty and Reginald, why?"

"They never call each other the same name twice. It's Rodger, and then it's Richard, and then it's Walter, and Henry, and Owen, and Bill. Don't you find that strange?"

"I don't think about it. They got into a car accident a few years back, and since that night they've always been just a little off."

"Trauma will do that."

"They didn't have trauma." Annie Mae went back to pacing.

"What do you mean?"

"The car blew up and there was glass and debris everywhere. It was a real mess. But they walked away without a scratch. They were fine. People called it a miracle and said they were blessed by God. Then, suddenly, Mom didn't want to go to church anymore. I think it freaked her out to think God may have blessed her. They're fine, though, just a little strange, calling each other different names and little things like that."

"You're sure they're fine?"

"Yes?" Annie Mae's eyes prodded at Fawhikwuff.

"What if, and just hear me out here, but what if two demons from my world took the place of your parents and have been disguised as them ever since?"

"No."

"It's just a thought, Annie Mae."

"Well, it's a terrible one."

28

210 DAYS, 12 HOURS, 58 MINUTES, 53 SECONDS, AND COUNTING TO CONQUER A PLANET

"So, let me get this straight," Perlicudak started, back in the demon-world pub, talking to a few of the locals. "Fawhikwuff, the tentacle demon, has teamed up with a couple of young human children—little girls, in fact—and they're now selling cookies?"

"The prize for selling the most is getting to meet a human who's going to the moon," answered a demon so green he nearly glowed. He nodded at his own comment and took a swig of his drink.

"So, his plan to beat me is to sell cookies?"

"No," Neon Green shook his head.

Perlicudak looked the other demon in the eye. "Then what is Fawhikwuff's plan? Or does he not have one?"

"Oh no, he's got a plan all right. It's pretty good stuff. Hey, maybe you should pair up with a scout child and start selling cookies, too!" Neon Green let out a laugh.

Perlicudak grabbed the demon by the neck and slammed the smaller creature down onto the sticky table. His face splashed in—something. "You think this is funny? Is your demon power being maddening? I will suck your spine out of your back and use it to clean between my toes if you don't tell me Fawhikwuff's plan!"

"Okay, Perlicudak." Pressed to the table, Neon Green forced out the words. Perlicudak loosened his grip so the demon could talk, but not so loose that the demon could escape. "His plan is to have the little girl win the contest. If she wins, he can possess her and then he can possess the astronaut she meets. If he possesses the astronaut, then he can hitch a ride with the humans to the moon. The moon is free of life, so once Fawhikwuff gets his bum up there, bing bang boom, Fawhikwuff has a planet, or something close enough to a planet, to win the bet you two got going, and you will have to do the chicken dance in front of everyone." He regretted including the last part.

Perlicudak let it go. "So, the girl is key. Without her, he's sunk."

"Maybe. I don't know. I guess so. Can you let me go now?"

"What is her name?" Perlicudak demanded.

"Whose?"

"The little girl, you sniveled-nosed demon."

"The little girl working with Fawhikwuff?"

"Yes, obviously her."

"Her name is Annie Mae. From what I hear, she lives in Virginia. I think that's how Fawhikwuff picked her. Her town is right out of the path to the human world."

"And she's working with Fawhikwuff willingly? He's not controlling her in any way, is he? This is by her own free will?"

"Yeah, man. She even summoned his bum back to her world when he tried to leave and give up. Remember that? It's like he's her servant, which is hilarious because, you know, he's this big, huge, scary demon and she's just this tiny, cute, little girl."

Perlicudak gave a sickly-sweet smile. "She's tethered to our world then, which means I can track her and find her, which means Fawhikwuff will lose."

"Why do you even care, man? You're like the most powerful demon we have ever seen. What's it gonna matter if Fawhikwuff wins or loses?"

THE NEXT DAY, neon green slime was found in a dumpster behind the pub. There were bones, but there was no spine.

29

209 DAYS, 12 HOURS, 04 MINUTES, 52 SECONDS, AND COUNTING TO CONQUER A PLANET

The snow was coming down harder by the minute. Annie Mae could hardly see the houses across the street through the blinding white. She told Fawhikwuff they typically didn't get so much snow, but he was glad they were. He had never seen snow before, other than in pictures. It was too warm in the demon realm to ever get any. And he figured there certainly wouldn't be any blankets of the soft crystallized moisture where he was heading at the end of his bet.

Fawhikwuff stretched out all six arms on Annie Mae's floor after she had gone downstairs to eat dinner. He tended to raid the kitchen at night and eat then. It wasn't as if he could just saunter into family mealtime. He had a feeling Annie Mae's parents wouldn't be a fan of his company, if they even noticed him.

Lolli earlier had trudged out the front door and back into the raging snowstorm to get to her own house. No one inside had offered her a ride or asked if she wanted to stay for dinner, which also struck Fawhikwuff as odd. Humans, as far as he knew, were supposed to be caring herd animals who looked out for one another's young. Were they easily manipulated? Sure. Could you turn them against each other for no good reason? Absolutely. But would they let a young girl brave the wilds of a raging storm without even batting an eye? Until today, Fawhikwuff would have said no.

Annie Mae's parents were off. There was something not right about them, and Fawhikwuff wanted to know what it was. But he wasn't about to let it distract him from his cookie sales.

30

209 DAYS, 00 HOURS, 49 MINUTES, 13 SECONDS, AND COUNTING TO CONQUER A PLANET

'Twas the night before Christmas, and Fawhikwuff was dreamin'. The Rumlereds, in bed, knew not of the demon.

Stockings weren't hung by the chimney with care. Holiday traditions weren't followed there.

Annie Mae was nestled all snug in her bed, and visions of cookie sales danced in her head.

Annie Mae's parents, after their tall night caps, were settled in for long winter's naps. Unknown to them, on their daughter's red carpet, nestled a demon who knew he was not well regarded.

Out on the lawn then arose such a clatter. Fawhikwuff jumped up. What was the matter?

Away to the window, Annie Mae flew like a flash. She tore open the curtains and threw up the sash.

The moon where Fawhikwuff so wanted to go, gave a luster of midday to objects below.

And what to the demon's and the child's eyes did appear? Well, it wasn't a sleigh and there were no reindeer.

Down on the lawn, melting the snow, was a fiery portal to a world unknown. Out on the lawn, another demon came through. It was the dreaded Perlicudak, his anger imbued.

With glowing big eyes, he looked to Annie Mae, a sickening smile and a tongue split, as long as the day.

Oh where oh where are parents when you need them? It seemed their nightcaps had done them in for the season.

More rapid than eagles, Perlicudak moved. And he shouted and whistled a sickening tune.

"Annie Mae, I am here to take you with me. You'll help no more demons for as long as you breathe."

To the top of the porch, to the top of the wall! Snowflakes that before the wild hurricane fly, when met with an obstacle mount to the sky.

Up to the housetop Perlicudak flew, with a mind filled with evil and with some chloroform, too.

And then in a rain of fire they heard, on the roof a demon clawed like a bird.

Fawhikwuff braced, protecting Annie Mae. But down the chimney the evil Perlicudak came.

He was dressed in all fur, from his head to his foot, and his clothes were charred and covered in soot.

A bundle of rage he held in his eyes, and he looked like a killer in reach of his prize.

His breath, how it stank! His fangs, how jagged! His droll little mouth dripped and was ragged. It was clear he had come, for one person alone. He reached out for her and let out a groan.

The stomp in his feet and the blood in his teeth, and there was smoke that encircled his head like a wreath.

He had a vile face; it was filled with evil. He couldn't be mistaken for an angry boll weevil.

He was lean and mean, a right jolly old demon, and Fawhikwuff cursed up a storm when he had seen him.

A wink of his eyes, he was nobody's pawn, and Fawhikwuff knew he wanted Annie Mae gone.

He spoke not a word, but went straight to his work; he knocked out poor Fawhikwuff with barely a jerk.

Positioning his hand to cup his ear, he tore up the stairs, his mouth in a sneer. He sprang to her room and grabbed her away. They flew to the snow, but not to play.

Too late, Fawhikwuff awoke with a start, heard Perlicudak leaving, heard his large fart. Then he heard words that rang like a bell. "Merry Christmas to you; you're going to Hell!"

Fawhikwuff yelled back; it was one great bellow. How could he have been bested by such an evil fellow?

31

208 DAYS, 23 HOURS, 59 MINUTES, 48 SECONDS, AND COUNTING TO CONQUER A PLANET

"You're coming back again?"

"Yes! Now will you please just summon me so I can get there quickly?" Fawhikwuff was on the phone and knew he was being short. Hesdihe didn't deserve it, but Fawhikwuff didn't have time right now to worry about his best friend's feelings. Not with Annie Mae in danger.

"Is that really your best use of time?" Hesdihe asked. "I mean, come on, Fawhikwuff, your clock is ticking. Can't you just kidnap and possess the second-highest seller and use her to win? Or, better yet, just hang out where the prize will be given and possess whatever little girl comes to collect? You can forget cookie-selling altogether then."

"I'm not possessing Courtney and helping her win, and I don't want to forget cookie-selling. I want to crush Courtney and prove to that smug Chloe that she's wrong. I want to rub her nose in it. In everything!"

"Wait, who's Chloe? Is that another demon? Did you seriously pick another fight with another demon? One bet at a time, Fawhikwuff!"

"No, calm down. Chloe is a child, and I hate her guts. She is honestly worse than most demons. Like I would rather see some demons than her. Now, please summon me home so I can sue Perlicudak, that cheat. I'm begging here!"

"You're going to sue him? Seriously? Fawhikwuff, you have gotten way too invested in all of this. There's no way you can win a lawsuit against the most powerful demon ever."

"I won't lose. I'm in the right. Besides, I'm appealing to the Head Council."

"Fawhikwuff, your mom isn't going to help you."

"Hesdihe, she is my mom, and she will help. She doesn't want to disown me. She certainly doesn't want to see me go to Hell."

"Ah yes, the bare basics of being a parent: just don't disown your kids and don't want them to go to Hell."

"Oh, ha-ha. Joke all you want, Hesdihe, but I'm sure she'll get Perlicudak to put Annie Mae back where she belongs."

"And what of Annie Mae's parents? Are you leaving a note?"

"What sort of note should I leave? 'Hey, happy Christmas morning. I'm a demon, not Santa Claus, and I'm writing to let you know that I'm going after your missing daughter because another demon, the worst demon ever in fact, came and snatched her up, and I couldn't stop it! Whoops, sorry. Hugs and kisses. Signed, Your Roommate You Didn't Know You Had.' A note like that? No, Hesdihe, no note. Honestly, I don't think they're even going to notice she's gone. The next cookie-selling meeting is on January 6th. We're out of cookies anyway, so if I get Annie Mae back before that meeting, we won't even lose any selling time. But that means I only have eleven days, so I really can't waste any time getting there. So, please, please would you please just summon me?"

"You know a demon isn't supposed to summon another demon. I could be sent to Hell for twenty demon days if anyone found out."

"So don't let anyone find out. This is important."

"So is me not going to Hell. I'm being serious. I could get into some real trouble."

"Hesdihe! It will be between me and you, and I'm not going to turn you over for doing me a favor. Now, if I say there was no summoning and you say there was no summoning, they don't really have enough to go on to charge you with anything."

"Just because we don't get caught doesn't make it any less illegal."

"Hesdihe!"

"Fawhikwuff!" Hesdihe replied in a mocking tone.

"Fine. Last year. Office party."

"You're cashing in that card now?"

"I am." Fawhikwuff nodded, knowing Hesdihe couldn't see him. Demons had telephones but were nowhere near video calling just yet.

"You only get to play that card once," Hesdihe warned.

"Yeah, I'm well aware. Now summon me."

"This girl must be really special."

"She's not. I mean, kind of, but like not in the way that phrase usually means."

"You make zero sense. But fine. I'm going to hang up now so I can summon you. Okay, Mr. Drama?"

"Sounds good. Thank you, Hesdihe."

"Yeah, whatever."

32

207 DAYS, 20 HOURS, 28 MINUTES, 39 SECONDS, AND COUNTING TO CONQUER A PLANET

"What took you so long?" Fawhikwuff demanded as he rematerialized in his old work office. Hesdihe's proud smile faded at Fawhikwuff's harsh words.

"I'm not really used to summoning things, seeing as it's illegal ever since Tenjad and Niratwaah used summoning to kill all those demons." Hesdihe turned slowly and casually in his swivel chair, his arms crossed, a slight glare on his face.

"Yeah, those two are awesome demons."

"What?"

"Nothing." Fawhikwuff laughed nervously and then noticed his best friend's sour face. "You okay? Is this seriously about breaking the law? No one will ever know. Though I do have to question your decision to use the office instead of your house just because, you know, privacy, and how freaked out you seemed to be."

"I guess you just haven't really been acting like a friend lately."

"What? Now? We're going to talk about our feelings now?" Fawhikwuff looked away, his initial exasperation turning to embarrassment as he considered how he'd been acting. "Okay, yeah, I'm sorry, Hesdihe. You're right. I haven't been very nice lately. I've been so stressed."

"I forgive you. We're good." Hesdihe uncrossed his arms, his face softening. "Now go win this bet so I don't lose you to Hell."

Fawhikwuff and Hesdihe shared a smile. "Thank you," Fawhikwuff said before vanishing into the dark night.

33

207 DAYS, 09 HOURS, 57 MINUTES, 32 SECONDS, AND COUNTING TO CONQUER A PLANET

"You have to be out of your mind."

"Well, that seems a little harsh. I'm not out of my mind. He took a little girl on the night before Christmas."

Fawhikwuff stood in front of four members of the High Council, his voice echoing off the meeting room's marble walls. The High Council members wore oversized black robes so all that was visible was dark fabric covering nondescript lumps. With the hoods up and faces covered, Fawhikwuff wasn't sure if his mother was among them.

Fawhikwuff hadn't seen his mother in years, but he would have hoped that if she was one of the four currently in the Demonic Temple, she would have said something. Instead, just one of the four spoke, and it was definitely not her.

There were twelve members in all, similar to a supreme court in the human world—except the High Council could dole out sentences so harsh Fawhikwuff, and nearly every other demon, feared the body, whether its gathering was full or in its initial committee of four. For Annie Mae, though, Fawhikwuff had decided to push away his fright and go to the temple uninvited to make his case. The council members just didn't seem to be grasping the severity of the situation.

"We are demons, are we not? Kidnapping the human young is often something we do, for many reasons," the talking hood said.

"But he didn't take her for 'many reasons.' He took her to rig a bet he made with me. We swore on the River Styx on that bet. If I lose, I have to go to Hell. I humbly request that you order him to put her back. She doesn't belong in our world."

"Well, did you both agree to play fairly, by a set of rules?"

"Uh, no."

"Then I think he is fully within his rights to kidnap a human child."

Fawhikwuff looked in disbelief at the hooded figures. One at a time he considered them, flabbergasted by their casual approach to kidnapping and rigging. Whatever happened to demon honor? Then he guessed what must be going on. Despite his better judgment he spoke again: "You all are on Perlicudak's payroll, aren't you?"

"No, Fawhikwuff," the hooded figure shot back quickly, swinging his head side to side, or what Fawhikwuff assumed was a head under there. For all Fawhikwuff knew, the council member could be shaking his butt. "You're seeing things that aren't there, Fawhikwuff. And you are making a very serious allegation. I warn you to tread carefully."

"Well, he has you under his thumb somehow." Fawhikwuff refused to back down. He pinched his eyes shut. If there was wrath to pay for what he was saying, he didn't want to see it coming.

He tried another tack: "What would make this an issue the council could help me with?"

"If you were to claim she was your child, or a family member of some sort, it would make Perlicudak's actions illegal, and he would have to hand her over to you. This will be difficult, though. Impossible probably. A demon parent and human child normally doesn't end well."

"She already has parents. Is there anything else I can do?"

"I'm afraid not, Fawhikwuff. Without her being family, this is considered a civil dispute between you and Perlicudak. We all wish you the best of luck in figuring out how to solve it on your own."

"Fine. I'll go talk to Perlicudak myself." Fawhikwuff said it as if it were a threat, but the council nodded in agreement, taking it as a brilliant suggestion.

"Good. Now, I can't speak for everyone, but I genuinely hope you figure this out."

34

207 DAYS, 09 HOURS, 57 MINUTES, 32 SECONDS, AND COUNTING TO CONQUER A PLANET

Fawhikwuff marched across town to the mansion district where Perlicudak lived. His, of course, was the biggest house.

With an odd sense of confidence, Fawhikwuff went right up to the front door and gave it a pound. Perlicudak cracked the door open, his tiny nose wrinkling at the sight of his newest nemesis. “Get off my property, Fawhikwuff. Your odor will make the grass green.”

“I’ll leave as soon as I get Annie Mae back.”

“Who?” Perlicudak sounded bored.

“Annie Mae.

“The name doesn’t ring a bell. Maybe you have the wrong house.”

“The girl you kidnapped in order to try to beat me in a bet that’s meaningless to you but scares you nonetheless. I actually might be the one who wins.” Fawhikwuff was practically growling. “It’s not going to work. You can’t just go and kidnap a human child. That’s not okay.”

“I’m not afraid of anything. And it looks like it did work, and I did kidnap her, and look at that, it doesn’t seem to be illegal, so, yeah, I heard about the council, I think I will get away with it." Perlicudak smiled condescendingly. "Look at you, Fawhikwuff. Every moment you're here pestering me is a moment your plan is failing and you move closer to losing a bet that means quite a lot to you. And when you do lose, it will be wonderful. You'll go to Hell and I won't have to deal with you ever again."

"You're cheating! You're breaking the demon code!"

"I'm just playing, Fawhikwuff. It's not my fault you let yourself make her a weakness. You love her."

"Ew. She's like two," Fawhikwuff spit in disgust.

"Not like that, you fool. My goodness, you truly are an idiot. You've fallen in love with her in the sweetest of ways. You see her like a daughter now, don't you? But truthfully, Fawhikwuff, she isn't yours. She never will be. If anything, I am doing you a favor here. You should thank me. You don't want to raise a human child. You can't even manage the child that is yourself. So, here's a bit of advice: When you get to Hell—you know, after you lose this bet—please grow up a little. For everyone's sake, okay?"

Perlicudak began to close the door, but Fawhikwuff blocked it.

"What are you doing?" Perlicudak demanded. "Shoo."

"I am going to save Annie Mae."

"She's not even here, you half-baked tuna melt. You think I would be foolish enough to bring her home with me? No. Now make like a tree and leave."

"I don't believe you," Fawhikwuff spat.

"That's because I'm lying." Perlicudak gave Fawhikwuff a humorless laugh and a rough shove, and he quickly slammed the door shut. Fawhikwuff stumbled back, fell off the front landing, and into the beautiful brown grass. He heard the lock click back on the porch and knew he wasn't going to be able to rationalize with the other demon. He wasn't going to get Annie

Mae back by asking, though he hadn't really expected to. Kindness, graciousness, and generosity were not traits Perlicudak possessed. He was a ruthless demon, and if Fawhikwuff was going to save Annie Mae, he needed to be smarter.

So, he decided to rip a page out of the oldest demon guidebook: enter without permission.

Fawhikwuff snaked around the side of the house, checking the basement windows until he found one unlocked. With a hard shove he pulled himself into the basement and hit the cold stone floor with a thump.

"Annie Mae?" he called out softly as he moved through the semi-darkness until he ran into a smooth wall. Gently he moved around the perimeter of the room until one of his hands found a door. He twisted the knob. As soon as the door opened, light flooded into the small space he was in and he saw he had been in a supply closet. The rest of the basement on the other side of the door was luxurious, a male demon's-only type of space. There were velvet chairs, trashy posters of famous female demons, and a polished mahogany bar. Fawhikwuff spotted about ten different bottles that each would sell for more than what he could make in a year working in the nightmare division.

Fawhikwuff felt a twinge of jealousy stab his chest. This was the demon's basement, and it was larger than Fawhikwuff's entire apartment. The leather, velvet, and fur throw pillows were nicer than anything Fawhikwuff had ever owned in his entire life.

Fawhikwuff didn't spend long feeling bad for himself, though. He spotted an elevator. Yes, an elevator. Not stairs. This wealthy demon kidnapper had an elevator in his home.

Fawhikwuff entered the small golden box with mirrored walls and examined the buttons. Despite the home only being three stories and a basement, each floor had two buttons — each floor number and "Point 1" and "Point 2"—which meant

Fawhikwuff was going to have a larger search than he anticipated.

"If I was Perlicudak, where would I put Annie Mae?" he whispered to himself. There was no way to know, so he just pressed "3" followed by "Point 2" and hoped for the best.

35

207 DAYS, 09 HOURS, 30 MINUTES, 32 SECONDS, AND COUNTING TO CONQUER A PLANET

The elevator was surprisingly quiet, carrying Fawhikwuff up—the only sound was the music of human voice cracks—until he reached his floor. The doors opened with an echoing chime. He saw he was in a large movie theater with a big white screen at one end and a snack cart at the other. Fawhikwuff helped himself to a Seven-Layer Despair bar as he looked beneath the seats.

"Annie Mae," he kept whispering, but he figured she wasn't there. A movie theater isn't really the ideal place for prisoners.

As Fawhikwuff munched on his candy bar, he checked behind the white screen. He found only bricks. There was nowhere to hide someone here. There wasn't even a projection booth at the back. The projector sat on a table instead, near where he had come in, loaded with a film reel called "Candy".

Fawhikwuff climbed back inside the elevator and pressed "3" and then "Point 1". An old Elvis song played softly this time as the car quietly slipped downward, its doors opening again with another loud chime.

He was in an enormous bedroom now. There was a sitting area and a bar in front of him. How many bars did this guy need? About halfway across the room were four steps leading to a raised platform where a massive bed, adorned with red satin sheets—of course red satin—was pushed against enormous picture windows. The amazing view was of the Pits of Hell. Fawhikwuff couldn't help but pause for a moment to take in so much beauty.

Fawhikwuff noticed two closed doors. A bathroom and closet, he figured.

"Annie Mae!" he called out, his voice a little louder now. He ascended the four steps and threw open the first door. Yep, a massive bathroom. That twinge of jealousy returned as he realized he could probably fit his whole apartment in Perlicudak's crapper. Imagine the party you could throw—in the bathroom!

Actually, he had never understood the appeal of a large bathroom. Just more to clean. Of course, Perlicudak, no doubt, had demon maids to do the cleaning. Still, so much extravagance for a room you just stink up and exit as quickly as you can. Ridiculous! He coveted it anyway.

Fawhikwuff opened the second door and found a closet nearly as large as the bathroom. An entire rack of human suits hung along one wall, none of them with the feminine hips like his Chris Green suit. These all looked like human supermodels.

Annie Mae wasn't here, either, and although he was enjoying his tour of all things he could never afford, he made his way back to the elevator. Two rooms down, way too many to go.

36

207 DAYS, 09 HOURS, 12 MINUTES, 23 SECONDS, AND COUNTING TO CONQUER A PLANET

He pressed "2" and "Point 2" and was taken to a museum of human torture devices.

It was dark, the only light being the glimmer of the moon dancing on the floor after bouncing off metal blades that hung on the walls, sealed in glass cases.

Man, this guy had it all. Some human nations had less weaponry than what he saw in just this one room.

It was creepy, actually. Most of the blades looked unused, and everything was so still. Fawhikwuff breathed in relief at not finding Annie Mae here, trapped in an iron maiden or hanging from one of the nooses secured every few feet to the ceiling like party streamers.

Fawhikwuff snuck back into the elevator and hit "2" and "Point 1". The doors slid shut and this time, instead of music, he heard children's screams. It was a good track, but considering Fawhikwuff's current predicament, he found it in poor taste.

The doors chimed open again, and Fawhikwuff realized immediately he was in trouble. There was a couch and, on the couch, sat Perlicudak. The homeowner's evil eyes bore into Fawhikwuff, causing his blood to curdle with fear.

"Fawhikwuff? Why are you in my house?" Perlicudak growled, springing to his, well, the closest word in human would be feet. He ripped off the headphones that had been blasting into his ears.

Fawhikwuff started pounding the elevator's "close-door" button, again and again. "Come on, come on," he muttered, but the doors were too slow.

Perlicudak slinked into the elevator with Fawhikwuff. Perlicudak's breathing was heavy, angry. He reached across and hit the "1" and "Point 1" buttons. The two rode down together, Perlicudak seething, Fawhikwuff shaking.

"You don't know when to leave well enough alone, do you, Fawhikwuff? I will be taking this up with the High Council—all twelve members. Yes, I can get a full hearing. Breaking and entering is a serious crime. And I will be handling this intrusion, this violation, in the proper way, unlike you. Once the High Council hears of this, everything will go through them, including if I was in the right to take Annie Mae, which we both know, deep down, I was, and which the committee of the council already confirmed. Unless I heard that wrong? No? Good.

"I suggest you go home, Fawhikwuff, to your shoebox of a home, and wait to be served a summons to appear. Sound good?"

Fawhikwuff nodded his head.

"Good. If I ever catch you in my house again, I will hurt you."

The doors chimed open one last time, and Fawhikwuff saw the front door. Perlicudak grabbed one of his arms and roughly tossed Fawhikwuff out into the night.

37

268 DAYS, 21 HOURS, 07 MINUTES, 39 SECONDS, AND COUNTING TO CONQUER A PLANET

"Why do you think the court is going to serve you your summons to appear here? You don't even work here anymore," Hesdihe pointed out, sitting at his desk, working on making a human in a nightmare dodge balls in a pit of fire-breathing snakes hurling insults.

Fawhikwuff was sitting at his old desk, but he wasn't working. "This is my last known place of employment. Demons go where employed during the day. They'd check for me here first; I just know it."

"You mean first, as in instead of your home, the place where you actually spend most of your time daily?" Hesdihe gave a little laugh. "Okay, Demon."

"This is all working perfectly, in its own way. I wanted to appeal to the High Council—"

"Who told you to go to Hell."

"—and now I get an audience with the High Council."

"You'll probably get Hell time."

"For what?"

"You broke into Perlicudak's house."

"He broke into Annie Mae's house. What's the difference?"

"There is a big difference. Annie Mae is a human. She has no rights here."

A knock on the office door startled both demons.

"Fawhikwuff?" It was a tiny demon, about half the size of Fawhikwuff, who wore spectacles larger than his head.

"That's me!" Fawhikwuff said excitedly.

The tiny demon passed him a folder, which Fawhikwuff took eagerly.

"You have been served!" The tiny demon announced before scrambling out and vanishing in a puff of smoke like a cheap magician.

"You must be the first demon to be excited to go to the High Council when you're not the one doing the suing." Hesdihe shook his head sadly and with a bit of disbelief at his best friend.

"Good."

38

205 DAYS, 12 HOURS, 26 MINUTES, 42 SECONDS, AND COUNTING TO CONQUER A PLANET

Fawhikwuff took in another deep breath, smelling the wonderful aroma of charred wood that filled the courtroom.

He was all alone at the defense table, eager to present his case and stop Perlicudak once and for all. He mostly just wanted to get Annie Mae back and head to the surface. They had cookies that weren't going to sell themselves.

"How does the defendant wish to plea?" the demon judge asked, the High Council sitting behind the bench. Members of the High Council came to every court case, but they didn't always weigh in. Fawhikwuff hoped they would this time and help him out.

He stood up, fidgeting at his tie nervously.

"I plead not guilty."

Fawhikwuff flustered as he heard Perlicudak give a short laugh from the prosecution table that sounded more like a bark.

"Um, not guilty under Demon Code Amendment 8, Section 20, line ninety-eight: 'A demon is allowed to enter another demon's home without permission if they believe it is to protect a family member'. I think Perlicudak actually was the one who put it best. Annie Mae is like a daughter to me. That's what Perlicudak told me. Then he kidnapped her, my daughter, and told me she was being held on the premises. I was trying to save her, after the High Council did nothing when she was taken."

Critical words of the High Council sparked an immediate buzz of murmurs and alarm throughout the chambers.

"Objection, your honor!" Perlicudak cried out, a look of bewilderment on his face as he glanced at Fawhikwuff. "You can only claim a family relation if both individuals, demon or otherwise, agree you are such. I did not go after his family; I went after a human girl he was working with. Since there is no record that Annie Mae has called Fawhikwuff anything more than a friend, Fawhikwuff can't claim her as family, and therefore he would not be protected under Demon Code Amendment 8, Section 20, line ninety-eight."

The judge turned back to Fawhikwuff. "Do you have any proof to support your claim? A drawing maybe? Human children draw sometimes, right? It's always awful work, but they keep doing it."

"I don't have anything like that," Fawhikwuff admitted.

"If he has no proof, then his claim is simply wasting the court's time," Perlicudak jumped in.

The judge shook their heads. "It's an easy fix, Perlicudak. You have to bring Annie Mae with you to court. We'll put her on the stand, and if she agrees that she and Fawhikwuff are family, the whole case is thrown out and Annie Mae will be protected under demon law as a member of Fawhikwuff's family. If she doesn't, then we start over, and Fawhikwuff has to come up with a new way to try to squirm out of this." The judge pounded a flaming hammer against the bench. "Court dismissed. I'll see you all back here tomorrow."

39

205 DAYS, 02 HOURS, 59 MINUTES, 16 SECONDS, AND COUNTING TO CONQUER A PLANET

"So, your entire case rests on the little human girl saying she sees you as a family member?" The barkeep slid Fawhikwuff another glass of tears. The cloudy liquid sloshed as it moved, making the glass slick to the touch.

"Yep." Fawhikwuff was feeling the weight of it all on all three of his shoulders. If Annie Mae said they weren't family, Hesdihe was right, he would be serving time in Hell for breaking into Perlicudak's house. He would run out of time. One reckless life choice, and he might end up in Hell forever, the thought of winning any bet a distant memory.

"My condolences. Your tears are on the house. I feel it might be your last."

"Yep. Thanks."

40

204 DAYS, 12 HOURS, 26 MINUTES, 42 SECONDS, AND COUNTING TO CONQUER A PLANET

"Court is now in session," the judge said before turning to the prosecution's table. "Perlicudak, where is the human child?"

"The human child refused to come, your honor," Perlicudak said. "And by Demon Code Article 2, Section 93, paragraph thirteen, if a family member will not defend their kin in a room of court, they are no longer considered to be family."

With begging eyes, Fawhikwuff looked up at the hooded figures behind the judge, the members of the High Council who had come to oversee the case. If his mother was one of the hooded, then, by demon law, soon she would no longer be considered Fawhikwuff's mother. He knew she wouldn't defend him. And that hurt most.

"What say you, Fawhikwuff?"

Fawhikwuff snapped back into focus as the judge addressed him. "Sorry, what?"

"Perlicudak claims since the child didn't show, you have no legs to stand on. What do you say in response?"

"That code only works if the child is of age, thirty-seven. Annie Mae is not of age, therefore since she is a child, whoever's custody she is residing in must bring her to court or face obstruction of justice charges. Perlicudak technically could be spending tonight in Hell."

All eyes shifted back to Perlicudak.

"Demons take longer than humans to develop, so I just thought—"

"Well, you thought wrong!" The judge cut off Perlicudak. "I'm not going to ask you again, Perlicudak. Bring the child tomorrow for questioning or you will be tossed into Hell for a sentence of thirty days."

"Thirty days?" A sly smile began to form on Perlicudak's lips.

"Yes, thirty days."

"Where would the human child go during that time?"

"She would become a ward of the demon state and be properly taken care of."

"So, Fawhikwuff wouldn't get her back?"

"Well, no. But you would be in Hell for thirty days and thirty nights."

"Which would prolong this case for thirty days?"

"Just bring the child in tomorrow, Perlicudak." The judge brought down the flaming hammer to signal an end to the day's proceedings.

41

203 DAYS, 13 HOURS, 27 MINUTES, 49 SECONDS, AND COUNTING TO CONQUER A PLANET

"Did you bring the child, Perlicudak?" The judge looked down from the bench, and a new day of proceedings began. It was clear Perlicudak hadn't. He clearly wanted the thirty-day sentence, because, with it, Fawhikwuff would be that much further behind in winning what had to be the stupidest bet known to demons.

"I have not, your honor." Perlicudak threw a smug grin to Fawhikwuff.

The judge opened their mouths to speak but stopped when one of the hooded council members leaned down and whispered one of their ears. The judge gave a nod. "You will serve thirty days in Hell."

Fawhikwuff objected immediately, jumping up. "Your honor! He's just trying to drag this case out. That's why he didn't bring her,"

"I will take my sentence. Thank you, judge," Perlicudak responded, still grinning.

"Let me finish," the judge barked, and the room fell silent. "You will serve thirty days in Hell *after* this case is closed. Your unwillingness to cooperate will not prolong this court case.

That wastes my time, and I don't waste time. For every day you fail to bring forth the human child, an additional ninety days will be added to your sentence. Do I make myself clear?"

It was Fawhikwuff's turn to flash the smug smile. "It seems perfectly clear to me."

"Your honor, that sentence is not what we discussed yesterday," Perlicudak argued, now the one springing out of his chair, anger seething in his eyes.

"The High Council has spoken, Perlicudak. I don't know why they want the two of you out of this courtroom as soon as possible, but—actually, I do know why. Perlicudak, you're a good demon, one of the best ever, but your attitude makes you unbearable to be around. No one really likes you; they just admire your work. And Fawhikwuff, what were you thinking? You picked a bet against Perlicudak? You are the dumbest demon ever. Both of you will make my life happiest when you leave my courtroom. So, yeah, I get why the council wants you out. Now, Perlicudak, head back to your fancy mansion and, tomorrow, bring the child. It isn't that hard."

42

203 DAYS, 09 HOURS, 39 MINUTES, 56 SECONDS, AND COUNTING TO CONQUER A PLANET

"The judge actually told Perlicudak that no one likes him?" Hesdihe burst out laughing. "Good for them. It's about time someone stood up to Perlicudak. And the judge is right."

"You should have seen his face." Fawhikwuff and Hesdihe were in Hesdihe's kitchen, eating takeout from the pub.

"I wish I could be there, I do, but there's no way I can get off work. I'd lose my job, and, unlike you, I'm not going to be ruler of the moon by the end of the year."

Fawhikwuff was silent for a moment before speaking again. "Do you really think I can rule the moon?"

"No, but you're very brave for not going down without a fight."

"Thanks. I think."

43

202 DAYS, 13 HOURS, 42 MINUTES, 19 SECONDS, AND COUNTING TO CONQUER A PLANET

"It appears Perlicudak is late." The judge sighed from the bench as another day of proceedings began. "As such, for failing to come on time, and for failing to bring the human girl today—"

"Annie Mae," Fawhikwuff corrected, then realized he had cut off the judge. He slowly looked up to see the judge glaring down at him.

"And for failing to bring 'Annie Mae', his sentence in Hell is raised to—"

From the back of the courtroom, with a dramatic bang, the doors burst open and Perlicudak entered, a squirming Annie Mae slung over his shoulder, a cloth sack over her head. She screamed to be put down and demanded to know where she was.

"Annie Mae!" Fawhikwuff jumped up. "Are you okay?"

"Fawhikwuff? Tell him to put me down!" Annie Mae screamed.

"Let her go!" Fawhikwuff ordered.

Perlicudak walked past Fawhikwuff instead and up to the bench. He set Annie Mae down on the charred spot where the judge tended to bring down the flaming gavel. He then went and took his seat, looking rather relieved to be rid of the young girl.

"Wonderful. Now we can continue," the judge said. "For being tardy, Perlicudak, your Hell sentence has been raised by twenty days."

"But that's fifty days in Hell! I brought her!" Perlicudak yelled.

"Look at that. Someone took basic math," Fawhikwuff said, the sarcasm thick.

"Do you want to make it fifty-five?" the judge threatened, and Perlicudak muttered something under his breath, but he didn't object.

"No," he answered sharply.

"Good. Next time, don't waste my time." The judge turned their attention to Annie Mae and removed the sack from her head. "Your name is Annie Mae, yes?"

"Where am I?" Annie Mae demanded, squinting, her eyes adjusting to the light.

"You are in demon court, Annie Mae. Very few humans ever come here. Nod if you understand me." The judge spoke kindly, the gruff tone used with Perlicudak and Fawhikwuff gone. The judge gently set a hand on the young girl's arm in a comforting, parental sort of way.

Annie Mae nodded yes.

"Do you recognize that demon?" The judge pointed at Fawhikwuff.

"Hi, Annie Mae," Fawhikwuff waved.

Annie Mae looked at him and nodded. A small smile formed on her lips.

"Who is he?" the judge asked.

"Fawhikwuff. He's a demon. He can sell cookies really well. He's going to beat Chloe and Courtney and everyone else. He's also going to conquer the moon."

Perlicudak scoffed. Fawhikwuff beamed.

The judge asked her next question: "Fawhikwuff claims you two are close. Is that true?"

"He stood up to Chloe when no one else would," was all Annie Mae said in response.

"Who's Chloe? Is she another demon?"

"No. A girl. A mean girl. She hates me because I'm different from other kids. She says I'm stupid and slow. She didn't think I knew what she meant when she used larger words while being mean to me and talking about me, but I did. I do. It's just that, when I read, the words jump around on me sometimes and I can get them wrong. That doesn't make me stupid. Also, I'm not a people person. That's what mama used to say. 'Just not good with people'. I keep up, though. I've only been held back once. I keep up in class. That's why Fawhikwuff made her cry. That's why I kissed her crush, though he always liked me better anyway. Chloe didn't ever see me as a real person until Fawhikwuff came and stood up to her. No one had stood up to Chloe before. We sell more cookies than her, too."

"Annie Mae, would you consider Fawhikwuff to be a member of your family?"

"He's not related."

"Not by blood, no. We demons believe, though, that family is more than just blood. We believe it to be deeper than that. Would you say Fawhikwuff is part of your extended family?"

A small smile grew on Annie Mae's lips. Her eyes locked with Fawhikwuff's and didn't leave them. She answered the judge with just one word: "Indeed."

44

202 DAYS, 07 HOURS, 02 MINUTES, 17 SECONDS, AND COUNTING TO CONQUER A PLANET

"We'll get you back home tomorrow, but for tonight you'll have to deal with my small place." Fawhikwuff led Annie Mae into his home. He immediately regretted that it smelled like old food and looked like, well, like a demon lived there.

After Annie Mae had said "indeed", the court had released her into Fawhikwuff's custody and care, and all charges had been dropped against him. Fawhikwuff was a free demon, but he was more excited that, now, Annie Mae couldn't be harmed by any demon ever again. If any tried to harm his family member, they would be instantly sent to Hell, which is where Perlicudak was going to be for the next fifty days, meaning he couldn't interfere with any of Fawhikwuff's plans.

"It's, um, small." Annie Mae said, looking around. Fawhikwuff was glad that was all she said about the dump he called home. But then she added, "I love it!"

45

201 DAYS, 20 HOURS, 26 MINUTES, 17 SECONDS, AND COUNTING TO CONQUER A PLANET

In the morning, Annie Mae and Fawhikwuff began their trek back to the human world. They walked day and night, Annie Mae often sleeping on Fawhikwuff's back, through the seven levels of deadly farts, through the sea of swirly-twirly broken hearts, and through a mind-numbing lecture before their journey landed them somewhere in the state of Virginia near Annie Mae's hometown.

"What are your parents going to say?" Fawhikwuff asked as he slipped into his Chris Green suit on the outskirts of town.

"Nothing good."

46

200 DAYS, 19 HOURS, 58 MINUTES, 47 SECONDS, AND COUNTING TO CONQUER A PLANET

Fawhikwuff, as Chris Green, and Annie Mae, as Annie Mae, stood outside the front door. "Should we knock? It's your house, right? Can't you just walk in?" Fawhikwuff asked.

"I don't know," Annie Mae said.

Fawhikwuff reached out and tried to turn the handle, only to discover it was locked. "Do you have a key?" Annie Mae shook her head. "Then I guess we're knocking." He pounded on the door.

Silence.

"I'll try." Annie Mae pounded on the door.

Silence.

"We could break a window and go in that way?" Fawhikwuff suggested.

"Mom wouldn't like that."

"Yeah, that's fair."

The door burst open then, and Annie Mae's mother stood on the other side with a light scowl. "Annie Mae, where in the dickens have you been?" Before Annie Mae could answer, the woman shushed her inside and turned back to Fawhikwuff.

"Thank you so much, young man, for finding her. We were just worried sick. Would you like to come in for something warm to drink?"

Fawhikwuff looked at the woman without answering. There was definitely something off about her, even if Annie Mae didn't think so.

"You ever hear of a demon pub?" Fawhikwuff asked, taking a shot and trusting his gut.

"A demon pub?" The woman's face faltered.

"Yeah, a demon pub."

"I'm not of the religious sort, sir."

Fawhikwuff slowly nodded. "It's not of this world."

Annie Mae's mother stopped moving, her hands going still and falling to her sides. She looked up intently, and her voice dropped two octaves. "What's your name?"

Fawhikwuff considered saying "Chris" but decided against it. "My name is Fawhikwuff, though I think you already know that. Don't you, demon?"

Annie Mae's mother stepped outside, closing the door quickly behind her. "Of course I do. Every demon knows your name right now. 'Fawhikwuff the Stupid' is mostly what I've been hearing. No offense. But what kind of demon makes a bet with Perlicudak? Especially one as outlandish as conquering a planet?"

"I was right about you." Fawhikwuff nodded his head, feeling a little triumphant. "You two are unregistered. You and your husband. You're hiding from the demon government, posing as Annie Mae's parents. Why?"

"Everyone has heard your name, but everyone has also heard my name and my husband's name."

"You're outlaws, using the kid as cover, because there are only supposed to be two of you, but with Annie Mae that makes three. Am I right?"

"You're smarter than most give you credit for, Fawhikwuff."

"What are your names?"

"Niratwaah and Tenjad."

"*You're* Niratwaah? Annie Mae's parents are Niratwaah and Tenjad? You guys are demon legends! Everyone knows how you took down that angel in Central Park and then had it grant you special powers. Tell me, are you two actually blessed by an angel? Are the stories true?"

Niratwaah, who still looked like Annie Mae's mother, offered a less-than-enthusiastic nod. Her head dropped. "It's a blessing and a curse for a demon."

"Why are you here in Virginia?"

"After the girl's parents died, we assumed their identities and have been able to live peacefully here ever since. You have no idea how many things out there are interested in demons blessed by an angel. So here we hide. Please don't tell anyone, Fawhikwuff, please! Why are you here anyway?"

"The little girl was just declared a part of my family in demon court. She's the scout who's going to help me beat Perlicudak. Me and her are going to sell the most cookies, beat Chloe, and then I'm going to catch a ride with an astronaut to the moon."

"Annie Mae isn't smart enough to do all that."

"She indeed is. She is winning, and she will keep winning. She is my golden goose, and I'm sick and tired of people saying she's not good enough. And why? Because she needs a little more help in school? Because she doesn't like reading? Maybe if people didn't label her as different or as stupid, from the first grade on, she'd be doing better. Maybe if she had real parents here helping her. No offense. But she's not stupid; she is smart. She just needs a little help sometimes, like we all do from time to time."

"You're going to get us caught, you know. All of us."

"Then I suggest you skip town, Niratwaah."

PART III

JUST THE TWO OF US

47

LEAVE IT TO THE RELEASE

Annie Mae's real parents had been dead this whole time.

The demons posing as her parents took off that very night without a word or a note or anything to Annie Mae or Fawhikwuff. It was too risky for them to stay. Fawhikwuff understood that, but he worried how the girl would take it when she realized her parents were just up and gone.

She seemed unphased, as it turned out. Were they really that awful at parenting? Or perhaps she overheard when Fawhikwuff learned the truth and was able to take time to get used to the idea. Whatever the reason, Annie Mae was still Annie Mae and was still her normal self, unburdened by their absence.

Bigger issues remained. Fawhikwuff and Annie Mae needed to keep selling cookies and fast. When school resumed after Christmas break, Annie Mae took every box of cookies she could get. Several of the other girls had begun giving their share of boxes to Annie Mae. They said they thought she could win and wanted to help her. They said they were proud of her.

Annie Mae had never seemed happier around her classmates. It was like she had finally found her place.

Her grades kept improving, too. The B's turned into A's. Even her English mark was on the rise.

Lolli said Annie Mae was like Rudolph the red-nosed reindeer, and that the girl needed to be more careful. When Fawhikwuff said he had never heard of Rudolph, Lolli tried to explain. "He's this reindeer, and his entire life he's been hated on because his nose is different. The second that his nose becomes useful to others, though, they let him in and treat him with respect. Think about it, Fawhikwuff, if the fog had never rolled in, would Rudolph's 'friends'ever become good people, who treated him nicely? Or, I mean, good reindeer or good elves or whatever?"

"Well, perhaps they only then realized how special Rudolph was?" Fawhikwuff asked.

"They don't think he's special. At least not special in a good way. They think he's useful. They use him. Reindeer aren't tools, though. They're like people, and I guess demons. They aren't here to serve your purpose. They're not here to benefit you. They're here to benefit themselves. If we didn't need to rely on others, if humans weren't social beings, we would all be a lot happier because we would never allow ourselves to be used. Rudolph wanted to be one of them, and, yes, he was happy in the end. But he was also being used by the very people who made him feel so small for so many years."

"And you think that's like Annie Mae's situation?"

"Yes."

"Well, then aren't you just like the rest of them? I was here at the start of the school year, Lolli. You two weren't friends. You started hanging out with Annie Mae only after I came and started standing up to Chloe."

That made Lolli think for a moment. "I'm like the elf, the one who wants to be a dentist and runs away from the other elves because he doesn't fit in with them, and partners with Rudolph. I'm an outsider, too, but less so than Rudolph because Rudolph can't pick a different nose. I'm a weak outcast, like Annie Mae. She helped me pull my head out of the snow and she gave me the courage to be like that elf and stop allowing myself to be put down. Obviously, being there from the start would have helped us both, but it didn't happen that way."

"What if everyone in real life is like the elf?"

"They're not."

"I think everyone feels like an outcast and wants to be let in and accepted."

Lolli had gone quiet before admitting she didn't know.

For forty-nine days, the trio lived in bliss with the cookies selling as quickly as supplies could be replenished.

But when day fifty came, they all knew that was the day Perlicudak would be released from Hell. They all knew he'd be angry. He couldn't touch Annie Mae, but that didn't mean he couldn't try to ruin things. They knew they had to be on guard.

48

151 DAYS, 19 HOURS, 28 MINUTES, 44 SECONDS, AND COUNTING TO CONQUER A PLANET

"A bike?"

"You have to learn."

"Do I, though?" Fawhikwuff looked down at the blue machine, his lips curling at the sight of such a contraption. He was in his Chris Green suit today, but that didn't mean he wanted to do human things. Annie Mae was holding out her father's bike to him while Lolli sat on the front porch, her legs crossed, a lollipop in her mouth. Fawhikwuff thought it was funny when Lolli ate lollipops, given her name, and the last time they had gone to the store, he had "convinced" the store owner to give them a large bag of Dum-Dums for free.

"You need to learn," Annie Mae insisted.

"Why?" Fawhikwuff continued to be stubborn.

"Cookie selling. The further we go the more people we have to sell to. This will help you get to them faster."

Fawhikwuff looked down at the bike again. She wasn't wrong. The few businesses in town had already bought so many cookies they could live on them alone for a month. Every person in town must have at least one case from Annie Mae. If they could go to the next town over, they could clean up there, too. There were new, albeit more distant, ripe pickings of weak and/or easily "influenced" humans.

Even still, Fawhikwuff wanted nothing to do with the bike. "You two can go sell in the next town over without me," he announced. "I don't want to ride the bike."

"We can't sell them without you. You know that," Annie Mae insisted. "Please, Fawhikwuff?"

"She's right," Lolli added, removing the lollipop from her red-stained mouth with a literal pop. "We need the demon influence. We need you to tell them to buy. With you, no one can say no. It's like magic: demon magic."

"So, I have to ride a bike?" Fawhikwuff sized up the wheeled death trap as both girls nodded their heads. Fawhikwuff let out a large huff of air. "What if I just run alongside you two? As a demon, I can move faster than a bike."

"Yes, because running as fast as a bike wouldn't draw attention to you at all. Come on, Fawhikwuff, think," Lolli said, popping the pop back in her mouth.

"Fine," Fawhikwuff grumbled. "Teach me."

49

151 DAYS, 17 HOURS, 46 MINUTES, 09 SECONDS, AND COUNTING TO CONQUER A PLANET

The next town over was about the same size as Annie Mae's town. It was also just as boring. The downtown was one block lined by storefronts. Houses filled in the streets surrounding downtown. A large factory sat on the edge of town, puffing dark smoke and providing jobs for people. Annie Mae had no idea what they manufactured in the factory. Fawhikwuff had asked.

It was a quiet and dark city. Although it hadn't rained and there wasn't a cloud in the sky, the people hurried about as if in a downpour, their hoods up and their eyes down.

"These people look like they need cookies," Fawhikwuff said with a smile at the two young girls. They were about to sweep, and they knew it.

50

151 DAYS, 17 HOURS, 39 MINUTES, 52 SECONDS, AND COUNTING TO CONQUER A PLANET

The trio entered the first shop on main street, a small bakery and café with seating in front. A strange feeling struck Fawhikwuff the moment he stepped in, right on the back of his Chris Green suit, at the neck. He turned back, slowly, but there was nothing there. The girls were already at the counter with a case of coconut cookies.

"Perhaps you girls don't understand how a bakery works. You buy cookies from me, not the other way around," the store owner said with a smile, trying to be polite as she told the girls to buy something or leave.

Fawhikwuff turned away again to examine the street outside, the uneasy feeling only growing stronger, like a weighted blanket on his shoulders.

Then, outside Fawhikwuff saw them, two gentlemen in trench coats and sunglasses. They were looking at the bakery—and, through the window, at him and the girls. Fawhikwuff watched as the gentlemen passed a folder between them. Then they left in opposite directions, in no hurry.

"Faw- Chris!"

Fawhikwuff turned toward Lolli's voice. "What's wrong?"

"Don't you have anything to say to the nice bakery lady who said no?" Lolli asked and nodded toward the counter.

"Oh, right. Yeah, sure. Sorry."

51

151 DAYS, 05 HOURS, 22 MINUTES, 46 SECONDS, AND COUNTING TO CONQUER A PLANET

"Did you see those weird guys outside the bakery today?" Fawhikwuff asked Annie Mae later, placing a plate of spaghetti noodles drenched in white sauce in front of her before grabbing his own. He preferred the food he made, but he missed having the demon version of Annie Mae's mom doing the cooking instead. This way was just so much more work.

Annie Mae shrugged and began digging in. Fawhikwuff wasn't the world's best cook. He was getting better as time went on, though.

"The one passed the other one a folder. They kept looking at me. Looking at us. I can't help but shake the feeling there was something off about them."

"Do you think they were demons?"

"No, that wasn't it. They were human," Fawhikwuff said, sitting down behind his plate.

"We sold a lot of cookies!" Annie Mae changed the topic.

"Yeah, we did. Sold out again. The next town over was a great idea."

"And the bike?"

"That was terrifying," Fawhikwuff deadpanned, making Annie Mae smile all the more. Fawhikwuff couldn't stop thinking about the two men in trench coats, though. "I wonder if those guys were like Russian spies or something. We can't let the Russians win this space race. If they do, why would NASA keep going? Then me and you would both lose, and that can't happen."

"I could still sell the most cookies."

"Well, yeah, sure, but there wouldn't be a prize or anything, so what would be the point? We would all be under Russian rule then, and I'd go to Hell for losing the bet." He wondered which would be worse.

"Could I hide you here?"

"No. If I lose and don't go through with my half of the deal, then every day I avoid it, another square inch of my body would feel like it's being bathed in holy water until I die from the pain."

"So, holy water is bad?"

"To us demons it is. It's like acid to us, and even more terrifying is that it can be made out of any water if a priest is present and willing to offer the blessing. That's why demons aren't a huge fan of priests. It really hurts, so why risk it? Priests don't mind us not coming by, either. It's a mutual stay-away deal."

"No more priests. Got it."

"Not for me at least."

Annie Mae nodded her head.

52

146 DAYS, 10 HOURS, 36 MINUTES, 12 SECONDS, AND COUNTING TO CONQUER A PLANET

As the troop leader rambled on about who knows what, Fawhikwuff, back in Annie Mae's body, made spitballs and flicked them into Chloe's hair. That morning, Annie Mae and Fawhikwuff had talked and decided to have Fawhikwuff possess Annie Mae for the day. Chloe had begun getting nastier again for reasons Fawhikwuff hadn't understood—until that boy in their class who Chloe apparently had a crush on but who had kissed Annie Mae instead greeted him, thinking he was Annie Mae. Chloe had looked over at them like she wanted to rip Annie Mae's eyeballs out and force feed them to her.

Chloe's hair was so bushy, she hadn't noticed the spitballs as they collected. So far, Fawhikwuff had gotten eight spitballs in without her noticing. Eight little white dots.

Flick! Make that nine.

"Cookie sales are higher this year than ever before!" Ms. Bratwurst exclaimed with a large grin on her face, as if she was getting a cut of the profits.

Flick. Ten.

"The nice folks over at NASA are so excited to meet whoever the top seller will be."

What a lie that was. Did she seriously think a bunch of astronauts, who are working to get to the moon, were excited about meeting some little girl who sold cookies? If they were, someone should alert Officer Big Nose. I mean, come on, going to the moon versus cookie sales? There was no comparison for the astronauts. For the girls, on the other hand, it meant the world. If you were to survey all the scouts in the room, selling cookies would have been a slam-dunk winner over beating the Russians.

Flick. Eleven.

"Annie Mae has a wonderful chance of winning this competition! She is up over a hundred boxes on the second-place holder. So as long as she can finish strong, we'll get the honor of knowing someone who got to meet a real-life astronaut! I think I speak for everyone when I say, Annie Mae, we couldn't be prouder of you."

Flick. Twelve.

"Now, girls, I have even more exciting news. We have been invited back to the cabins eleven days from now because of Annie Mae's and Chloe's amazing sales performances. Chloe is still substantially behind, but she is the tenth-top seller nationally, which is just wonderful! I mean, it's not nearly as good as Annie Mae, who remains in first, but it is still a large accomplishment. Chloe, you should feel very proud of yourself."

Flick. Thirteen.

Flick. Oops! Fawhikwuff missed, and it landed on the center of the desk, right in front of Chloe. Spotting it, Chloe screamed, jumped to her feet, and pointed at it in horror. She spun on Fawhikwuff, and her shock turned to rage.

"You! You threw that spitball at me, Annie Mae!"

Lolli began to laugh, noticing finally the other thirteen spitballs stuck in Chloe's hair. Soon the entire troop was laughing.

"Prove it," Fawhikwuff said with a smile.

"Chloe, dear, you may want to excuse yourself and fix your hair," Ms. Bratwurst suggested.

"Why? Isn't Annie Mae in any trouble here? Why does her selling cookies suddenly make it so she can't be punished?" Chloe placed a hand on the back of her head then and felt what everyone else was laughing at. She looked as though she might throw up as she ran out of the room, the other girls' chuckles playing her out.

"One more thing, ladies, before I completely lose your focus. There are a few gentlemen here from the government who would like to talk to each of you today before you head home."

Through the classroom door sauntered the two men Fawhikwuff had seen out in the street when they had gone cookie selling at the bakery.

Uh-oh.

53

146 DAYS, 10 HOURS, 02 MINUTES, 53 SECONDS, AND COUNTING TO CONQUER A PLANET

"Name?"

Fawhikwuff, in Annie Mae, had been led to a smaller classroom. The two men in suits sat on the other side of a desk. Fawhikwuff was suddenly very glad he was in charge today.

"My name is Annie Mae. Who are you guys?"

"We are with the government. We are here from Area 51. We investigate the peculiar, the otherworldly, and any unnatural phenomenon. We are here investigating a tip we received about a threat to our great nation. We shouldn't take up too much of your time." The man doing the talking pulled out a folder that looked an awful lot like the one Fawhikwuff had seen the men passing between them in the street. From the folder the man pulled out a picture and slid it across the table. It was Fawhikwuff in the Chris Green suit.

"Would you mind telling me who this man is?"

Fawhikwuff picked up the photo. "This is Chris. He's a family friend." Fawhikwuff passed the picture back.

"Is he a friend of your mom's or your dad's?"

"Yes. I mean, he's friends with both." Fawhikwuff was

bending the truth, but he was answering confidently, and he wasn't about to say the guy actually was friends with a couple of twelve-year-old girls. That could get Chris arrested—or worse.

"How did your family meet Chris?"

"He's a big supporter of cookie-selling."

"He helps you sell cookies for the scouts?"

Fawhikwuff paused for a moment. The men had seen him in the Chris Green suit selling with Annie Mae and Lolli. It would be foolish for him to try to lie about that. "Yes. I find it helpful to have an adult present when I go out to sell."

"Has Chris ever threatened anyone when you two were out selling."

"No."

"Has Chris ever attacked anyone?"

"No! Why would you ask that?"

"We have reason to believe Chris is a Russian spy, a dangerous individual."

"What?"

"I know this can be upsetting, Annie Mae, and I'm very sorry for that. But this is also very serious."

"What you are accusing Chris of is slander."

The two men exchanged a glance Fawhikwuff couldn't read. The one doing all the speaking turned back first. "Has Chris ever done anything strange or unexplainable?"

"Strange how?"

"Anything that you feel is unnatural. Maybe shape-shifting, vanishing?"

Those were common practices of demons. These men weren't looking for Russian spies, they were looking for demons. "No, of course not." Fawhikwuff had gone back to lying. Did the government somehow figure out what he was? If it wouldn't give him completely away, he would have used his abilities to figure out what they knew.

"Have you ever seen Chris's skin off his body?"

"Ew! No!" But of course, he had. He had stored that skin in Annie Mae's bag for the longest time. He had used Chris Green's mouth to hold books and money for so long that when he put the suit back on, there had been an odd papery taste in the mouth. For a few months, the Chris Green suit was more a purse than a disguise.

"Do you know anything of Chris's background?"

"He's from Florida." Florida? Where had that come from? Fawhikwuff was just proud for having come up with a plausible answer so quickly. But why Florida?

"Has Chris ever asked you to do anything you didn't want to do? Has he ever threatened you or your parents, making any of you do something you wouldn't normally do?"

"No. Can I go now?"

"Just one more question. Does the word 'Fawhikwuff' mean anything to you?"

"No," was all he said, though, now, he was the one who felt like throwing up.

54

146 DAYS, 09 HOURS, 48 MINUTES, 16 SECONDS, AND COUNTING TO CONQUER A PLANET

"What's your name?"

"Lolli."

"That is your birth name?"

"Yep. Read it and weep, boys. My name is cooler than yours," Lolli answered, leaning back in her chair, studying the government officials before her.

The men exchanged a smile. "We are with the government. We're here from Area 51 investigating a tip. We won't take up much of your time. I am Agent Johnson, and this is my partner, Agent Neilson."

"Area 51? Alien catchers. Sweet."

Agent Neilson pulled out a photo and held it out. Lolli recognized it instantly as a picture of Fawhikwuff in the Chris Green suit.

"Lolli, do you know this man?" Agent Neilson asked.

"That's Faw- Chris," she said, catching herself.

"Faw Chris?" Agent Johnson asked.

"Chris. His name is Chris. Sometimes people call him Father Chris. Yes, that was what I was getting at with the Faw. He used to be a priest, but he, uh, left the priesthood for a woman. Then the woman broke his heart. Real, real tragic stuff."

"Does Chris help you sell cookies?"

"No more than any other grown man." Lolli tried to smile, but it did nothing to soften the agents' gruff exteriors.

"Has Chris ever threatened anyone when you were out selling?"

"Oh yea- I mean, no. Definitely not. Never would threaten anyone. Chris is the sweetest guy you will ever meet. You know how priests who are no longer priests are."

"Has Chris ever attacked anyone?"

"What is this about?"

"We have reason to believe that Chris is a Russian spy, a dangerous individual."

"Oh, no. He's really not."

Johnson wrote something down. It all felt so intense to Lolli as she began to bounce her leg, tightening her arms around her. Then it was Agent Johnson's turn to speak again. "Has Chris ever done anything strange?"

"No stranger than any other adult."

"He hasn't done anything you feel is unexplainable? Shape-shifting? Vanishing? Manipulating?"

"No, not that I've seen."

"Has Chris ever requested you do anything you didn't want to do?"

"No."

"You're doing really good here, Lolli." Johnson offered a smile. "We just have one more question for you and then you can run home, okay?"

"Okay."

"Does the word Fawhikwuff mean anything to you?"

"No," Lolli said, but perhaps a little too quickly.

55

146 DAYS, 08 HOURS, 40 MINUTES, 32 SECONDS, AND COUNTING TO CONQUER A PLANET

"What is your name?"

"Chloe. Now, who are you and what makes you think you can keep me here? When my father hears of this, he will see to it that you both get fired."

The men exchanged a smile. "We are with the government. We're here from Area 51, in order to investigate a tip. We won't take up much of your time. I am Agent Johnson, and this is Agent Neilson."

Agent Neilson pulled out the picture of Chris and passed it to Chloe. "Do you recognize this man?"

"No."

"Are you sure?"

"I think I would recognize a man with those hips," Chloe scoffed, passing the photo back. "Can I go now?"

"Just a few more questions. I promise we are making this as painless as possible. We don't want to be here with you, either. Now, are you sure you don't recognize this man? Perhaps he has come to pick up Annie Mae?"

"This has to do with Annie Mae? That girl is stealing the

win from me in cookie-selling. It's not fair. It's like this year she grew a brain."

"What do you mean?"

"I mean, Annie Mae could barely talk to people when this contest started. Now we're all supposed to just believe she can sell all the cookies? Please."

"We have reason to believe this man may be helping Annie Mae."

"So, she's cheating? I knew it."

"No, she's not cheating; she's simply using *abnormal* resources."

"Oh. I was hoping she was cheating. Then she would be kicked out. Can I go now?"

"One more question, Chloe. Does the word Fawhikwuff mean anything to you?"

Chloe went silent for a moment, thinking. "I think I heard Annie Mae and Lolli say it once or twice. I don't know what it was about, though."

"Thank you, Chloe. That is exactly what we needed."

56

146 DAYS, 06 HOURS, 56 MINUTES, 27 SECONDS, AND COUNTING TO CONQUER A PLANET

"Why is the government looking for you? What did you do?" Lolli demanded. Lolli and Annie Mae sat at the kitchen table while Fawhikwuff cooked dinner. They were having pasta—again—because that was the human food Fawhikwuff cooked best.

"I don't know," Fawhikwuff answered. "I didn't even know your government knew about demons. I mean, come on, how many bad breaks are we going to get?" He sprinkled some red pepper flakes over the dish.

"You should keep being me." Annie Mae studied Fawhikwuff for a reaction. "You should, until they go away. It would be safer."

"As much as I appreciate that, you do still need to go to school. Otherwise, you're going to fall behind with your grades when it's time to go back to being you, and our top goal is still to sell the most cookies. You need to win the contest, and I need to beat Perlicudak."

"Perlicudak must have tipped them off," Annie Mae grumbled.

"I mean, that would make sense," Lolli agreed. "He can't

come for you and Annie Mae directly anymore, so he sics the government on you."

"We don't need to worry about that right now." Fawhikwuff scooped up three dishes and served them. "Shall we offer a prayer for our meal?" He held out two of his hands for the girls to take. They did, and he led them in prayer. "Dear Heavenly Father, protect these children and bless that I stay out of the pits of Hell. Dear Satan, if you ever leave your prison in Hell, we'll ask you to bless our meal, too. Dear Heavenly Father again, please allow the seasoning in this dish to be to your liking and protect us from poison. Keep Satan locked away in Hell and give out poison in his drink. Amen."

"Fawhikwuff, you have the weirdest prayers," Lolli said, letting go of his hand so she could dig in.

"Would you prefer your food poisoned?"

"Why would it be poisoned? You cooked it!"

Annie Mae began to laugh, and soon all three were laughing until Annie Mae spoke again. "If they know your name, can't they summon you? We were able to, and we're just kids." Fear danced in her eyes.

"Annie Mae is right," Lolli agreed.

"I don't know," Fawhikwuff admitted. "But I know it won't help anything if we sit here and fret instead of eating."

57

146 DAYS, 05 HOURS, 32 MINUTES, 18 SECONDS, AND COUNTING TO CONQUER A PLANET

"Fawhikwuff?" Annie Mae's urgent but loud whisper came from the living room, where the girls were watching something with an annoying laugh track; Fawhikwuff had no idea what and didn't care. He was in the kitchen washing dishes. He tossed the towel aside and hurried through the plum-colored hallway and into the next room.

"They're watching us," Annie Mae said, still softly, both girls hunkered down low.

Fawhikwuff slammed the curtains shut.

"What if they saw you in the window before you did that?" Lolli asked, taking in Fawhikwuff's demon form.

"I don't know," Fawhikwuff whispered back, "but these guys are going to be an issue."

"What happens if they take you?" Annie Mae turned around and looked at Fawhikwuff. "I can't live alone."

"You can come and live with me," Lolli said with a smile.

"What about your parents?" Annie Mae asked.

"I'll just say it's a sleepover, and then you'll never leave. You'll be fine. And Fawhikwuff is going to be fine, too. He'll beat 'em up, right Fawhikwuff?"

The girls both looked at Fawhikwuff.

"If they summon me, I have no choice in going. But I will always come back. And if they are dumb enough to confront me straight on, we will beat them. We will get through this."

Annie Mae peaked her head through the curtain, looking one last time at the two scary looking government men watching them from their car parked across the street.

58

144 DAYS, 08 HOURS, 23 MINUTES, 16 SECONDS, AND COUNTING TO CONQUER A PLANET

"Hello, ladies!" Ms. Bratwurst greeted the girls with her usual painted-on smile. "Today's meeting is going to be a little bit different. You all remember Agents Johnson and Neilson, yes?"

While the rest of the troop gave small affirmative noises, Fawhikwuff, as Annie Mae, leaned forward, ears piqued. Annie Mae was terrified of the government men, and Fawhikwuff didn't blame her. They freaked him out, too, though he tried not to let Annie Mae see it.

"They want to tell you a little bit about what they are looking for, in hopes that if you see something, you'll know enough to notify me so that I can let them know," Ms. Bratwurst explained as the two men entered the classroom. When Fawhikwuff had been questioned, he hadn't realized how tall Agent Johnson was. He had to duck through the door, and he loomed large over the seated scouts.

Fawhikwuff felt a knot in the pit of his stomach. This wasn't okay. He needed to leave. He needed to get away from these men, not invite them in to lecture. His fear was amplified by

Annie Mae's as his eyes darted to the door and then to Lolli, who gave him a concerned look. His heart was beating faster. Could he make a run for it without being caught?

"Hello, ladies," Agent Neilson's sickly-sweet stare landed on Annie Mae. "We are looking for someone who doesn't belong here in the beautiful U.S. of A. They may look like us, they may talk like us, but make no mistake, girls, they are not one of us. And they are not to be trusted. One false move and you may fall into their traps. They want you to believe they are friendly, that they are one of us. They want you to believe they are on your side and that they will keep your best interests in mind. They won't. They are evil, vile creatures who will say whatever it takes in order to save their own skin."

"Yes, ladies, we are talking about the Commies." Agent Johnson picked up the narrative, but Fawhikwuff wasn't listening anymore. He could hardly hear over the sound of his twelve rapidly beating hearts, all pounding in a deafening chorus of fear and worry. They weren't talking about Commies. Fawhikwuff was smart enough to know they meant demons. Specifically, him.

They knew. He didn't know how they knew; perhaps Annie Mae was right about Perlicudak tipping them off. Really, it didn't matter how, but they knew.

"They disguise themselves as friends, and then they use you to get what they want," Agent Neilson continued. "They are, inside, nothing short of a monster. They go against God and what he stands for. They go against everything you believe. They will latch themselves onto you, and they will bleed you dry, until you have nothing left to give except your life, and then they will take that, too. They will destroy all of us. We are lucky to have a lead on one man who we believe is a Commie and who is right here in your town. In your homes perhaps. In your lives. Rest assured, we will not stop until we catch this man, but we need your help to do that."

Fawhikwuff looked at the door again. It was only about ten feet from where he sat. He could make it before they could. He could run. But then what would happen to Annie Mae? What would happen to her if he made her look guilty? He couldn't do that. He would sit, hearts pounding, blood rushing, mind clouded, and he would be stronger than he thought he was. He would persevere and he would get Annie Mae out of this mess he had put her in.

"The man we are looking for goes by the name of Chris," Agent Johnson took up the torch of speech. "He is invested in the cookie sales. We believe he plans to use the winner of the cookie-selling contest to get close to the men going to the moon. We believe he plans to destroy our rocket, ensuring that the space race is won by the Russian Commies."

"His real name is Fawhikwuff." It was Neilson's turn again.

"That's a Russian name?" The girl who puts her feet up on the desk snickered.

Before either agent could answer, Fawhikwuff's stomach lurched. Annie Mae's form pitched over, throwing up a green mush of pasta and other food. When had she had peas? With a second heave, the stomach was emptied. Fawhikwuff felt a hand and looked up to see Ms. Bratwurst trying her best to be comforting.

"Come, Annie Mae, let's get you washed up," Ms. Bratwurst said and looked around the room. "Lolli, will you go to the bathroom with her?"

"Yeah, of course," Lolli said, getting to her feet and gently guiding Annie Mae around the vomit puddle on the floor.

Before they left, Fawhikwuff heard Ms. Bratwurst tell the men, "You must forgive Annie Mae. I think your words of a traitor just upset her so much that it had to come out some way. Talking of spies is upsetting for all of us."

"Of course," Agent Neilson said. "We'll have to apologize to her *personally* later."

"That's so sweet of you."

Personally? Fawhikwuff felt like puking again.

59

127 DAYS, 08 HOURS, 31 MINUTES, 49 SECONDS, AND COUNTING TO CONQUER A PLANET

Over the next two weeks, the government men watched and followed the trio's every move. They weren't good at going unnoticed. Or, perhaps, the men wanted Fawhikwuff, Annie Mae, and Lolli to know that they were there, waiting and watching for a mistake so they could seize them.

Not until Fawhikwuff, as Annie Mae, and Lolli boarded the bus for the out-of-town scout camp did they seem to shake free of the men. The two girls wiped clean circles on the bus's grimy back window so they could look for the men's long, waxed-to-a-shine black car, which had become omnipresent whenever they were out selling cookies, lurking like a cat or grim reaper. They didn't see it now, though.

"Maybe we lost them," Lolli said with hope.

"Or maybe they're just meeting us at camp. They know where we're going."

Lolli shrugged and joined the group of girls singing about taking down beers and passing them around. No one questioned why there were beers on the wall in the first place.

60

127 DAYS, 02 HOURS, 31 MINUTES, 49 SECONDS, AND COUNTING TO CONQUER A PLANET

The camp seemed colder than on their previous visit, and it wasn't just the chilled air. There was something else. The girls seemed more serious, like everyone realized that all the top sellers were here, that the end of the contest was coming, and that, soon, only one of them could be the winner.

"Come on," Lolli said, linking arms with her best friend. They had a plan to ensure Fawhikwuff and Annie Mae could both be at camp together. Lolli led them to the troop leader. "Ms. Bratwurst, I mean Ms. Bauhaus, Annie Mae and I need to use the bathroom. We'll be right back. Okay?"

"Fine, dear, just hurry." The troop leader seemed frazzled and only half listening.

Lolli and Fawhikwuff made their way to the woods behind the outhouses. Hidden by the trees, Fawhikwuff left Annie Mae's body, freeing the girl once more and leaving Fawhikwuff in demon form. He suddenly wished he had packed the Chris Green suit. "So, in this brilliant plan, what exactly am I doing?" Fawhikwuff asked.

"You're keeping watch and making sure the government dudes don't come for us," Lolli explained.

"In the woods? Behind the outhouses? Where I have zero sightlines?"

"That way no one can see you, either. You can't come out looking like that, and your Chris suit doesn't really work here, or anywhere anymore since you're wanted for being a Commie." Lolli smiled, but Fawhikwuff was regretting going on this adventure.

"You guys don't need me here. I'll just make my way back to the city."

"We will need you if the government dudes attack. Besides, that's way too long a walk on your own without a disguise," Lolli said.

"I'll pick up a hitchhiker."

"No," Lolli pressed. "Just stay here, Fawhikwuff. Come on, Annie Mae, we have the welcome meeting."

Annie Mae gave a small smile before Lolli dragged her away toward the welcome cabin.

61

127 DAYS, 14 HOURS, 22 MINUTES, 16 SECONDS, AND COUNTING TO CONQUER A PLANET

Fawhikwuff was doing a pretty good job of staying hidden, though he hated it. He felt like he was just sitting around doing nothing. He knew, though, that, right now, he couldn't be selling cookies. He just hated feeling so useless.

His mind wandered. Perlicudak couldn't win this bet, he decided, not just because Fawhikwuff feared being sent to Hell but because Perlicudak was a mean bully. And bullies shouldn't win. Fawhikwuff didn't want Annie Mae to see a bully win. That wasn't how things were supposed to work. That wasn't how the world was supposed to work. Sure, in nightmares that Fawhikwuff made, oftentimes the bully would win and the dreamer would be wedged into a locker or sliced open like a piece of fruit, and the bully would go free. But those were just dreams. This was reality. This was Annie Mae's life.

"Let me go!"

Fawhikwuff snapped to attention at the shout coming from camp. Fawhikwuff sprang up and bolted through the woods, dry twigs snapping under his tentacle-like "feet."

"Let me go!" The shout came again as Fawhikwuff eased to

the edge of the woods. There, in front of him, were two government officers handcuffing Annie Mae. The troop leader was yelling at them, but she was being drowned out by the agent reading Annie Mae her Miranda rights and Annie Mae screaming for them to get off her.

Fawhikwuff's blood boiled. He weighed his options. If he ran in there, that would throw away any chance of winning the cookie-selling contest and winning the bet. If he didn't, though, it appeared Annie Mae would be arrested, and they still wouldn't win anything. Also, he would have to break her out of whatever jail they put little girls who hide demons in.

Fawhikwuff's choice was made for him by Agent Neilson's next words. "Come on, Fawhikwuff," the man grunted, pulling Annie Mae upright. Whatever was going on, she was being arrested because of him. They must think she's a demon, which was fair, considering the amount of time he had spent as Annie Mae this year.

Fawhikwuff stormed out of the woods. "Let her go!" he screamed. "It's me you're looking for."

Everyone turned and saw Fawhikwuff. Their jaws dropped. Their mouths hung agape. Screams echoed into the night. Girls scattered like ants after their hill gets stepped on. One girl jumped in the lake to get away. As if demons couldn't swim.

"No!" Lolli screamed. "Fawhikwuff, run! *Run!*"

Ms. Bratwurst fainted.

Fawhikwuff didn't blame anyone for their reactions. He was supposed to look terrifying. If he didn't scare humans, he wouldn't be a very good demon. Fawhikwuff also didn't care about the little girls and prissy troop leaders. The one face he truly cared about smiled at him.

"Fawhikwuff. So we finally meet," Agent Johnson said, looking unphased at the sight of a real demon. "I am Agent Johnson."

Agent Neilson, still holding tightly onto Annie Mae, introduced himself as well. "We're from Area 51," he finished, as if Fawhikwuff hadn't met them before.

"My name is Fawhikwuff. Release Annie Mae. She's just a child. It's me you want. Let her go."

Agent Neilson took a step closer to Fawhikwuff, dragging Annie Mae with him. "You like her?"

"As if she were my own child."

"How? How did you two even meet?"

"I needed someone who was going to win at selling the most cookies. That was Annie Mae. She's a winner. You can see that just by looking at her. She has fought her whole life, and she is winning."

Agent Neilson looked at Agent Johnson. "The prize for selling the most cookies is to meet an astronaut." Agent Neilson turned back to Fawhikwuff. "You want to meet an astronaut? That is what this is about? You kidnapped a defenseless little girl to meet an astronaut? Are you working with the Russian government?"

"Um, I'm obviously working with Annie Mae, not any Russians. And please get this straight in your tiny little brain, Agent Neilson, I didn't kidnap anyone," Fawhikwuff argued.

"I think she has Stockholm syndrome," Johnson said. "I say we take her back to her parents and explain the situation."

"You can't. They're gone," Annie Mae said defiantly.

"Whose gone?" Johnson asked.

"My parents are gone."

"Did Fawhikwuff make them disappear?"

"No, of course not."

"Were they killed?"

Annie Mae looked at Fawhikwuff as if she were trying to remember something he would know. "I don't know," she finally admitted.

Fawhikwuff spoke up. "Her parents were replaced by two demons currently on the run from our government. I met them when I first came into Annie Mae's life. Apparently, the notorious couple killed Annie Mae's parents years ago and assumed their identity. I rid Annie Mae's home of that vermin and have been looking after her myself."

"We'll have to call foster care then," Agent Neilson said to his partner, who nodded in agreement.

"What's that?" Fawhikwuff asked.

"You don't need to worry about that, Fawhikwuff. Trust me, once you get back with us to Area 51, it will become the least of your concerns."

"I'm not going back to Area 51," Fawhikwuff argued with a shake of his head.

"You have two options here, you slimy demon, and I don't think you're going to like either very much. Frankly, if I was in your shoes, I know I wouldn't. But I'm not a demon lowlife like you. Your first option is to come peacefully with us. Once on base, we can give Annie Mae visiting rights and for as long as she chooses you can see her. You'll be locked away, but you'll have some rights. Option number two is that you run, flee for your miserable life. We can't catch you on foot; and in case you haven't noticed, we are surrounded by woods that would make 'on foot' your best option. You run, you evade arrest, and we have constant surveillance on Annie Mae. She will never have a normal life. And when we catch you—and yes, we will catch you—you will be dragged back to Area 51 and you will have no rights. You will never see Annie Mae again. The choice is yours, demon."

62

127 DAYS, 12 HOURS, 57 MINUTES, 38 SECONDS, AND COUNTING TO CONQUER A PLANET

Fawhikwuff didn't fit well in the back of the men's car, as stretched and long as it was. While waiting to be taken away, he could still hear Annie Mae and Lolli screaming, demanding his freedom. But he had made his choice. Not that it mattered. No matter what he picked, this was it for Annie Mae's cookie sales, meaning she wasn't going to meet an astronaut. Meaning he wasn't going to the moon. He had fewer than one hundred and fifty days before he had to go to Hell for losing a stupid bet, and he'd rather spend those days where Annie Mae could visit him, if she wanted. He wanted her to have a normal life. This way, both she and Lolli would be safe and okay, even if he wasn't.

Fawhikwuff lowered his head into three of his hands in frustration. How had they been careless enough to allow this all to happen? Why hadn't he taken Hesdihe's advice on other ways to win his stupid bet? Then Annie Mae wouldn't be in danger. She never would have been almost arrested in front of everyone. He wished he had had enough time or a way to erase this from the other girls' memories so he could save Annie Mae the embarrassment. He had really screwed up this time.

That's what he felt the worst about, putting Annie Mae in danger just to win a stupid bet. As much as he wanted to avoid Hell, it wasn't worth the girl's life. She deserved better than him.

Suddenly the shouting outside stopped.

Fawhikwuff figured the two girls must have given up. That was for the best. The agents weren't going to let him out; Fawhikwuff knew that much. Lolli and Annie Mae screaming their heads off would only accomplish them getting into trouble, too.

There was something off about the silence, though.

It was too silent.

It wasn't just that the girls had stopped screaming, birds had stopped chirping and the wind in the trees couldn't be heard. Chloe's shrill, know-it-all voice wasn't even piercing the background anymore. Everything was perfectly silent.

Something was wrong.

Fawhikwuff's first worry was that Perlicudak was dumb enough to be here. Perhaps the other demon was just that stupid, though.

But then the back door sprung open next to him and standing there he saw a cloaked High Council member.

"You have disappointed me," the council member said, lifting her hood and revealing her human suit, which was that of a twenty-something-year-old blonde woman who looked as though she could slay both men and a fashion show.

"Mom? Hey!" Fawhikwuff said after recognizing the voice. "Nice human suit. You are looking really good."

"From the dawn of time, we have, for the most part, kept our existence a secret. Now here you are, giving us away and getting us all in trouble." She passed him a human suit she had been holding.

"Thanks, Mom," Fawhikwuff muttered, stepping out of the vehicle and slipping into the suit. He was taller now and had better hair. He wore a pair of glasses halfway down his human nose, and his button-up shirt's sleeves were rolled up just past the elbows. All in all, he liked this suit better than his Chris Green suit. He looked both like an accountant and an athlete.

"We're going home now," his mother ordered.

Fawhikwuff looked over at Annie Mae and Lolli's frozen forms. His mother had stopped human time in the general area so she could bring him home, so she could rescue him. Fawhikwuff had never seen a time-freeze so strong, so universal. Even mosquitoes and birds were frozen mid-flap.

He wished he had been better, for Annie Mae's sake. He had forced her demon parents out, saying they weren't good enough, but he didn't feel like he had been much of an upgrade.

"Son, we're going home," his mother repeated.

Fawhikwuff looked back at her. "I know."

"We have to clean up the mess you created."

Fawhikwuff looked back at Annie Mae. Her face was all scrunched up, and her mouth was opened wide, a frozen scream wanting to leave her lips. He had never seen her so angry. Lolli looked about her normal level of outrage, which was high. He had tried so hard to be there for both of them, but, in the end, he hadn't helped either of them.

"She'll be fine," his mother assured him, following her son's stare. "She's a smart girl, even if the humans can't see it. You found a good ally, and that's hard to do in the human world. She'll be fine. It's you with all the issues."

"I only have one issue," Fawhikwuff said, turning back to his mother as he tried to push his failings out of his mind. "Perlicudak's bet."

"We'll discuss that, too, once we're home."

63

136 DAYS, 22 HOURS, 12 MINUTES, 38 SECONDS, AND COUNTING TO CONQUER A PLANET

A newspaper was slammed down on the table in front of Fawhikwuff so he could see the front page. He was in a courtroom again, but this time it was just members of the High Council standing around the defense table, where he sat, their eyes glaring at him, letting him know he was in serious trouble.

"I look pretty good in this picture. They got my good side and really captured my essence, you know, all that I am as a demon." Fawhikwuff offered a weak smile in an effort to lighten the mood. No luck. He picked up the paper and looked again at the image of him at the troop camp being confronted by government agents.

"This is not a joke!" a member of the High Council yelled at him.

"I know. I know it's not. I'm sorry."

"You have exposed our existence to the humans!"

"I am aware of the severity of my actions. Again, really, really sorry."

"Are you? Because from our end, it looks like you and Perlicudak are playing a dangerous game without thinking about how it might impact the rest of us. The humans know you now, and this Area 51 business will not go away until they are satisfied. Do you understand what you have done? You have put us on the human's radar, and not just the desperate or weirdo ones trying to contact the dead or the devil."

"Yes, I realize and understand all of that." Fawhikwuff was careful not to look directly at any of the council members.

"If you weren't going to lose your stupid bet, we would be sentencing you to Hell ourselves. You have done nothing but bring dishonor to all of us!"

"What do you want? What can I do?" Fawhikwuff snapped as he looked up. "I can't change what happened. I screwed up. I was trying to protect Annie Mae, but I get it, I screwed up. I can't change that. So, what do you want from me? To just feel bad? Well, congratulations, guys, I feel terrible. I couldn't be there for the one person who believed in me. Bravo to me. Job well done." Fawhikwuff stormed toward the door.

"Fawhikwuff, we're not done here yet." His mother's voice froze him. But only for a moment.

"I am," he growled and slammed the door shut behind him.

64

136 DAYS, 03 HOURS, 28 MINUTES, 13 SECONDS, AND COUNTING TO CONQUER A PLANET

"I brought pub food!" Hesdihe smiled, trying to sound cheerful, as Fawhikwuff opened his door.

Fawhikwuff smiled back, completing the charade and letting his friend inside. "Good. I'm starving."

The two sat down in the living room and opened the bags of food. Hesdihe had gotten all their favorites: eyeballs on intestines, despair juice, soul soup, marinated garlic brain bread, and chicken nuggets.

"I have missed food like this," Fawhikwuff said, digging in. "I mean, human food is fine, but this stuff, this is the good stuff."

"I couldn't agree more," Hesdihe said with a smile that was real this time. "So, what's the plan, Fawhikwuff? You're just going to throw a pity party until the girls decide to summon you back, like you're their missing little puppy?"

"Ha-ha, you're so funny. No, that's not the plan. Annie Mae is family now. I'm going back, but I can't land in Virginia in the same spot. My guess is Agents Johnson and Neilson will still be there watching Annie Mae and waiting for me. I need a different human suit, and I'm thinking either little old Gladius

Haugen or the one my mother gave me. I was actually mapping out a new route when you came in." Fawhikwuff pulled a map off the floor and showed it to Hesdihe. "See, if I take this path through the valley of severed eyeballs and then head down through Michigan, I should land in Indiana. From there I just have to head east."

Hesdihe nodded, checking the route before looking at his friend. "Last time you gave up. What's changed?"

Fawhikwuff looked back at the map. "I guess I did."

65

135 DAYS, 11 HOURS, 29 MINUTES, 05 SECONDS, AND COUNTING TO CONQUER A PLANET

Backroad diners serve the best food. That's what Fawhikwuff learned as he made his way cross country, "persuading" waitresses along the way to give him meals for free. He didn't view it as violating his powers. Perhaps he should have, but a demon has to eat, and it wasn't like he had human money. Gladius may have looked like a grandma that would give you one dollar for every year on your birthday, but she was actually super broke.

Departing another diner, Fawhikwuff swiped a newspaper. It read like gossip. "Fawhikwuff: Where is He Now?" screamed the lead headline. He hadn't grabbed the paper because he was on the cover, though. He had grabbed it for the sidebar story: "Annie Mae Moved to Psych Ward."

He had an address now.

Annie Mae had been moved to a children's psychiatric hospital about two hours from her home city. It was called Goose Pine Home for Children. The story said it was a nice place. That was good, but he was going to bust Annie Mae out anyway, and then they would be on their way. That girl was going to meet an astronaut, no matter what. That was the least he could do for her.

66

126 DAYS, 08 HOURS, 32 MINUTES, 55 SECONDS, AND COUNTING TO CONQUER A PLANET

There she was.

From where Fawhikwuff was hiding in the bushes, he could clearly see into one of the second-floor windows of Goose Pine Home for Children, and sitting in a chair in all white and a tan sweater, looking out the window with dead eyes, was Annie Mae. She looked doped up to a near comatose state. She was there, physically, but not so much emotionally or mentally, Fawhikwuff feared.

Seeing her like that broke all twelve of the big demon's hearts. She looked sick, her face pale, her eyes staring blankly.

Fawhikwuff leaned back against the bush, breathing hard, the threat of tears stinging his eyes. She was a child, and he was an adult, even if he was a demon; it was his job to protect her, and he felt like he had failed.

He couldn't just storm in there in the daylight. There were several guards posted around the perimeter, no doubt watching for him. Why else would the military guard a facility for children, right? If Fawhikwuff had learned anything, it was that society didn't seem to care about kids. Not enough to pay the military to stay and protect them, that was for sure. He would have to keep watch and break in when everyone was asleep. Then he could safely get Annie Mae.

He looked back at her one more time and regretted not sending her away from him when he had the chance.

67

125 DAYS, 23 HOURS, 32 MINUTES, 55 SECONDS, AND COUNTING TO CONQUER A PLANET

Fawhikwuff was surprisingly light on his feet and quiet for such a large creature.

He wanted Annie Mae to recognize him, so he had left the Gladius suit outside in the bushes.

With ease, he scaled the wall up to the second-floor window where Annie Mae had been a few hours earlier. He had waited until all the room lights had flicked off before attempting the daring rescue.

He gently popped the window out of its frame and set it down on the cool wood floor inside the room. He slinked in, folding himself so he could fit through the smaller-than-he-expected opening.

Walking past little girls in their beds, he wondered if Hesdihe was controlling any of their dreams, or if they could dream at all with all the medications they were given.

"Annie Mae?" Fawhikwuff whispered into the dark, but not a child stirred as he continued to scan the beds.

Then he spotted her, sleeping like an angel in the bed closest to the door, a pink sheet stained with brown blobs tucked up under her chin. Fawhikwuff reached down, using all six of his hands to gingerly pull back the sheet and to lift Annie Mae out of the bed. She curled into him comfortably and didn't wake up.

"Let's go home," he whispered to her, a smile on his face. She was safe now. He would make sure of it.

"Indeed." Her small voice came so softly he wasn't sure if she said it or if he imagined it. Either way, he couldn't help but smile warmly.

"MONSTER!" a child's blood-curdling scream shattered the otherwise-peaceful room. Fawhikwuff turned and saw a small girl on her knees in bed, pointing in his direction.

"MONSTER!" she screamed again.

"No, I'm not a monster. It's fine. I'm fine. Go back to bed!"

"MONSTER!" she screamed a third time.

Another child awoke and started screaming, too. She didn't scream "monster!" or any other word. She just screamed. Like an airhorn. Which was way worse, Fawhikwuff decided.

A light turned on in the hallway and snuck in under the closed door, as Fawhikwuff, cradling Annie Mae, leaped through the open window and landed in the soft grass below.

Fawhikwuff took off running at his top speed, grabbing his Gladius suit in one hand as he passed the bush and sped on.

He heard shouts in the night air behind him, but he didn't turn to look. There was no need. He had Annie Mae. That was all he needed. They were safe now. The humans could never catch a demon running, so long as he didn't follow any roads.

68

125 DAYS, 23 HOURS, 32 MINUTES, 55 SECONDS, AND COUNTING TO CONQUER A PLANET

Fawhikwuff climbed the front steps and grabbed the padlock securing the door. He squeezed it in his fist until it buckled and broke, freeing the door from a chain that hadn't been there the last time he had been. "There," he said with a smile.

"I don't think we're supposed to be here," Annie Mae whispered. She had awakened, and although her eyes were still glassy, her steps stumbly, and her words slurred, she was going back to being her again.

"It's your house. Where else would we go?" Fawhikwuff grinned, happier than he felt, as he opened the door for her.

Annie Mae entered the plum-colored hallway on hesitant feet. "What if we get caught?"

"We won't."

"How are you so sure?"

"I'll destroy them this time. If they come for you, they won't leave alive."

"No!" Annie Mae exclaimed, glaring at him, her night shirt fluttering around her ankles as she turned to face him.

"And why not?"

Annie Mae crossed her arms. "We agreed. No killing."

Fawhikwuff made a guttural, inhuman sound of protest. "Fine," he relented. "No killing the bad guys."

"No killing at all!"

"Fine."

"Thank you."

69

125 DAYS, 22 HOURS, 04 MINUTES, 46 SECONDS, AND COUNTING TO CONQUER A PLANET

"There." Fawhikwuff beamed at the meal he had prepared. He set it on the table. There hadn't been a lot left in the house that hadn't spoiled, and he was proud of what he had been able to pull together.

Annie Mae pushed the noodles around with her fork.

"I was thinking." Fawhikwuff broke the silence. "Since we're both technically on the lam now, we could just scope out the NASA gates the day the winner gets to meet the astronaut. You know? Then I could maybe just possess the winner and insist on you coming with her because we're totally besties or some crap like that, and then I take over the astronaut, go to the moon, say it's mine, and stuff. You know? And then you come home with me."

"Home where?"

"In, uh, Demon Land."

Annie Mae wasn't sure, and her face didn't mask her uncertainty. "I'm a human, though."

"You'll fit in; don't worry."

Annie Mae shook her head. "We should team up with Chloe."

"Chloe?" Fawhikwuff thought Annie Mae was joking or maybe there was some other Chloe he didn't know about. Then he saw the look on her face. "You seriously want to team up with Chloe? Your Chloe? Your bully and your school's number-one mean girl? That Chloe?"

"Calm down, Fawhikwuff. Last I heard she was number ten in sales. We could push her over the top."

"She's also the one who has tormented you every day. Why would you want her to win? I'd rather we just kill her."

"No! Come on, how many times do we have to talk about that?"

"I know, I know, we're not killing her or anyone else, yadda, yadda, yadda. But still, Chloe? As a partner?"

"She already knows us," Annie Mae argued, "and she can be nice when she wants to be. She just rarely ever wants to be. If we team up with Chloe, we can win. You can win your bet. Then we can go home."

Fawhikwuff made another guttural and inhuman noise before finally giving in. "Fine. We partner with—I can't believe I'm saying this—we partner with Chloe."

70

125 DAYS, 20 HOURS, 38 MINUTES, 16 SECONDS, AND COUNTING TO CONQUER A PLANET

How do you pick a stone to throw against someone's window to get their attention? If it's too big, you risk smashing the glass. If it's too small, you risk it never making it there.

"Are you sure this is Chloe's house?" Fawhikwuff asked Annie Mae as his eyes searched the dark ground for just the right-sized stone or pebble.

"Yes." Annie Mae pointed once more to the window she knew belonged to Chloe. "I wish you would have worn your Gladius suit," she muttered.

"Gladius doesn't have much of a throwing arm," Fawhikwuff argued.

They needed to talk to Chloe, but it wasn't like a demon, not even one dressed as an elderly woman, could just ring the doorbell, accompanied by a missing child, and say, "Hello, I'm here to talk to your young daughter." Yeah, that wouldn't get them anywhere except locked up. A pebble to the window was their best bet.

Fawhikwuff located a small stone and threw it as gently as

he could at the window Annie Mae told him belonged to Chloe. It bounded off with barely a noise.

"This isn't going to work," Fawhikwuff muttered.

"If I went to school, I could ask her there," Annie Mae offered.

"You'd be sent back to Goose Pine before you could even get a word in. Do not go to that school." Fawhikwuff picked up another pebble. He threw it a little harder this time. It banged off the window, making a much louder "ting" sound.

"Again," Annie Mae ordered.

Fawhikwuff threw another, and a moment later a light turned on in the room. "She's awake."

"Throw another."

Fawhikwuff picked up yet another stone and tossed it up. It struck the window with a bolder "tink" sound, and the window opened. Chloe emerged and glared down. "Annie Mae? What are you doing here?" Then her eyes widened. "And oh! My! God! What is that thing you are with?"

"I have a name, Chloe," Fawhikwuff called up.

"Fawhikwuff, right?" Chloe was putting it together and her voice softened again. She actually smiled, guessing why they were here.

"Right," Fawhikwuff nodded.

"Well, what do you two want? What are you doing here?"

"How would you like to be the top cookie seller in the country?" Fawhikwuff asked.

The smile grew wider on Chloe's face. "Why? What do you get out of it?"

"We'd come with you to NASA to meet the astronaut."

"That's it?"

"That's it."

"I'm only number nine," Chloe said with a shake of her head. "There is no way we can win."

"Let's just say, my being a demon really helps with cookie sales."

Chloe nodded, grinning. "Fine. Let's team up."

71

125 DAYS, 12 HOURS, 38 MINUTES, 16 SECONDS, AND COUNTING TO CONQUER A PLANET

Fawhikwuff, as Annie Mae once again, waited outside Chloe's house the next day. It was a Saturday and they had arranged to go out and sell out of Chloe's supply of cookies. That should move her up to number eight, they figured. It was still a way off from number one, but they could make it. They had crunched the numbers. Chloe just needed to keep taking as many cookies to sell as she could.

Fawhikwuff knew they had to be careful around town now. Everyone knew what had happened. To disguise Annie Mae, they pulled her hair up into a high ponytail, very unlike her braid or the straight hair she usually wore. They also put dark sunglasses on her and tied a scarf around her head a little like Rosie the Riveter's. Annie Mae looked different, but Fawhikwuff was still nervous.

"I'm leaving!"

Fawhikwuff, who today was possessing Annie Mae, jumped at the voice calling from inside the house. The front door burst open then and out into the world came Chloe.

"Good!" A voice screamed behind her. "Get lost, you ungrateful child!"

"You would like that, wouldn't you?" Chloe yelled back.

"Stop shouting, Chloe! The neighbors will hear you!" the woman inside retorted.

"Right. I almost forgot that's all you care about!" Chloe slammed the front door behind her and hurried down the steps to the sidewalk.

"Hey," Fawhikwuff Annie Mae greeted.

Chloe looked confused. "Annie Mae? You look ... different."

Fawhikwuff Annie Mae looked down at Annie Mae's outfit. Apparently, they had done well. "Thank you, Chloe. Who were you just yelling at?"

"Oh, that's just my mom. It's no big deal. Let's go sell some cookies, yeah?"

"Are you sure you're okay?"

"Yes, I'm fine."

"All right. Let's go then."

PART IV

WE MIGHT ACTUALLY PULL THIS OFF! QUICK, KNOCK ON WOOD!

72

ESCAPING TO SUMMER

When news broke that Annie Mae had escaped the children's home with the help of a demon, rumors flew. A hastily organized religious vigilante group was formed and promptly burned down Annie Mae's house, bellowing that it was in the name of "justice" and had to be done to "chase the Devil out of town". Joke was on them though as Fawhikwuff was very much not the Devil. Demons can be so misunderstood.

Thankfully, Fawhikwuff and Annie Mae weren't at her house when it was set ablaze. When they did return that night and saw what happened, they went to Lolli's. Her ground-floor bedroom made a perfect hideout.

Chloe and Fawhikwuff, who looked like sweet little Annie Mae to everyone they approached, sold cookies like no one's business. Everyone speculated that Chloe's wealthy father must be behind her sudden sales spike. No one suspected for a moment she would partner with Annie Mae and a demon. No one suspected a demon was pulling up Chloe's case count. Of course, it would have been easier if Annie Mae could have just kept selling. Whenever Annie Mae was recognized, which despite the disguise happened more than Fawhikwuff would have liked, Fawhikwuff had to use his demon powers of manipulation to convince the humans they hadn't seen her.

Agents Neilson and Johnson came back and interviewed everyone again, but this time, they didn't find any proof of Fawhikwuff being back. When they had tried to scope out Lolli's house, thinking, rightly so, that Fawhikwuff and Annie Mae might go there, Fawhikwuff had snuck up behind them, and using his demon powers convinced them the best course of action would be to search for him and Annie Mae in Minnesota. The agents had left that night for the land of one-thousand lakes, and the selling of cookies continued.

Chloe slowly moved up in the sales ranking.

It was close to the finish line between Chloe and Courtney, and when the troop leader got the envelope announcing Chloe's win, everyone was overjoyed. Annie Mae, despite having had stopped selling, still came in third.

Fawhikwuff and Annie Mae were the happiest when Chloe told them the good news. In one week, they would be going to NASA to meet a man on his way to walking on the moon. All Fawhikwuff had to do was catch a ride and then he and Annie Mae would win to some degree.

As tense as Fawhikwuff and Annie Mae were, across the country, the humans were also waiting on pins and needles. In just over a week, Apollo 11 would launch. No one had any idea a demon would be on board. All they knew was that if they got to the moon before the Russians, they would officially win the space race, and that their great nation would remain the top superpower for decades to come. It was all so exciting.

"Can you breathe without oxygen?" Annie Mae asked Fawhikwuff one night. Fawhikwuff told her he could. He wasn't positive that he could, but most demons were able to, so he figured he should be fine if something happened. Fawhikwuff would be fine for the few moments he would be on the moon.

It was the underdeveloped technology the humans had that worried him most. Demons were already using cell phones, after all. Fawhikwuff himself had been using his to keep in touch with Hesdihe, who had been keeping a close eye on Perlicudak, in case the demon tried anything foolish to hurt Fawhikwuff's plans. So far, things seemed calm. But there's a thing about calm: It never lasts.

73

08 DAYS, 15 HOURS, 38 MINUTES, 19 SECONDS, AND COUNTING TO CONQUER A PLANET

"We're here," the driver, an older man with graying hair who worked for Chloe's family, called back.

Fawhikwuff, as Annie Mae, and Chloe were in the backseat of Chloe's car on the way to NASA. This was it. This was what he had been working for all year.

"Come on," Chloe said with a smile, not waiting for the driver as she opened her door. Outside the car was a woman wearing no expression, a sensible brown and tan business suit, and a tiny pair of eyeglasses on the tip of her nose. She carried a clipboard in one hand and a pencil in the other.

"Chloe?" The woman offered a terse greeting, and Chloe could have sworn she felt the temperature drop. "Welcome to NASA. Today you will be meeting Michael Collins. He'll be the command module pilot on Apollo 11, leaving on the sixteenth." The woman stopped talking as she saw another girl crawling out of the car behind Chloe. "I'm so sorry, but we are only prepared to have one child on base today. Your friend can't come. And will your driver be the adult accompanying you?"

Fawhikwuff overheard and walked Annie Mae's body right

up to the woman. "You're going to let me come, too. In fact, you'll see it as an honor. You have no idea who I am and you will have no desire to report my being here to anyone. Also, you're going to let us come alone, without an adult," he said, Annie Mae's voice dripping with demon manipulation.

"Of course, yes. You will be coming, too. It will be an honor to show both of you around. We're going to do a tour of the facility and then you will both get to meet Michael Collins."

74

08 DAYS, 15 HOURS, 21 MINUTES, 13 SECONDS, AND COUNTING TO CONQUER A PLANET

"Welcome," the stiff woman started as they entered the building. Fawhikwuff and Chloe exchanged a smile. The girls were led everywhere inside the sterile white building. It was filled with equipment, gadgets, controls, and nerds. Fawhikwuff loved every moment of it. They had eight days left to win his bet, and he was onsite ready to do just that. He was going to win. He was going to beat the famed Perlicudak. He could feel it.

"Here we have the control room, but we have to be quiet," the woman said, leading them into a large room with long control desks that faced an enormous screen. Everything was new and mysterious. Sure, Fawhikwuff had mobile phones and high-definition television in the demon realm, but demons weren't sending anything into outer space.

While Fawhikwuff remained riveted, Chloe seemed to lose interest after the first hour. When the tour ended, Fawhikwuff knew he needed to get back to work, needed to possess an astronaut, but part of him wanted the stiff woman to keep leading them around and showing him things. It was that cool!

"And that concludes the tour," the woman said, her voice

still an uninterested monotone. "Michael is going to talk to both of you now." She smiled, but it never made it to her eyes, as she opened a door to a long table and a man in a NASA-emblazoned jumpsuit sitting at the far end. Michael Collins, the man Fawhikwuff needed to occupy in order to travel to the moon, was waiting for them.

"Thank you," Chloe said, and the two entered the room, and sat down at the table with Michael. The door was closed behind them with a light thud as the stiff woman left.

The room was poorly lit and smelled musty. Fawhikwuff wondered if the small grimy windows in the room leaked, based on the scent.

"Hello, ladies, it's nice to meet you. My name is Michael Collins, and I have been training for a while now to go to the moon. I'm excited to answer any questions you may have." He extended his hand to them, and they each took a turn politely shaking it.

"It's nice to finally meet you," Chloe said with a small smile.

"It's nice to meet you ladies, too. Now, which one of you sold the most cookies in the country?"

"That would be Chloe," Fawhikwuff answered, flashing the cutest Annie Mae smile he could muster.

"And what's your name?" Michael asked the little girl who spoke.

"I'm Annie Mae."

"Well, it's lovely to meet Chloe and Annie Mae. Now, do you young ladies have any questions about space or space travel?"

"I think Annie Mae wants to know a lot," Chloe said with a knowing smile.

"Well, go ahead then, Annie Mae."

"Thank you, Michael. I guess my first question is," Annie Mae paused for a moment, "have you, Michael Collins, ever been possessed before?"

"Excuse me?"

"I asked if you, Michael Collins, have ever been possessed before."

"Um, no, I don't think so." He let out a nervous laugh.

"Oh, you would know."

"I suppose I would." Michael's jaw dropped. He was both baffled and horrified. "Um, do you girls have any space- or astronaut-related questions?"

"I might on the rocket," Fawhikwuff replied with a nod. "But not now."

"No, I'm sorry, I think there must be some confusion. You ladies aren't going to be going on the rocket."

"I will be," Fawhikwuff said, a sly grin crossing Annie Mae's face. "I will be there more than you will be there."

"I think this little meet and greet is over." Michael Collins stood. "If you'll excuse—"

"Oh no, sir, this is just the beginning."

75

08 DAYS, 12 HOURS, 21 MINUTES, 16 SECONDS, AND COUNTING TO CONQUER A PLANET

"You don't stand like he does." Chloe sounded just like a fidgety mother primping and prepping her precious child for a school concert as she considered Fawhikwuff's possession of the astronaut Michael Collins.

"He's so tall. What is this green bean, five-foot-ten? Five-foot-eleven? He's taller than my Chris Green suit, I think," Fawhikwuff commented.

"So, what now?" Chloe asked.

Fawhikwuff stopped staring at his Michael Collins form and looked back to Chloe and Annie Mae. "Right. The plan. Definitely have one of those. Well, you two will have to leave. Michael Collins made it clear you won't be seeing the rocket, which is fair, so you can't exactly stick around without raising suspicion. Anyway, you'll be gone, and I'll follow orders until liftoff. I'll go to the moon and, after Buzz and the other one plant the American flag, I'll say I need a minute. Then, once they're back on the rocket, I'll cut the video feed, and then I'll rip up the American flag and claim the moon as my own and win the bet."

"No," Annie Mae said.

"No?"

"For once, I actually agree with Annie Mae," Chloe concurred. "If you cut the feed, how will we know if you actually did it?"

"Well, it's a demon promise, so once the time on the bet runs out, either I will be sent to Hell and be in immense pain or the curse will make Perlicudak do the chicken dance in the demon pub in front of everyone. You don't have a choice about following through, which is probably the best part. We don't need to humiliate you humans by showing that their exploration to the moon was ruined by a demon."

"I want to see. We should get to see," Chloe said, crossing her arms defiantly.

"Then I won't be able to catch a ride back to Earth. There's no way the humans are going to let the rocket land with a known demon on board."

"Learn to fly the rocket yourself then," Chloe ordered, as though it was that simple.

"Yeah, that's more something Hesdihe would do—could do," Fawhikwuff answered.

"Who is Hesdihe?" Chloe asked.

"And, more importantly," Annie Mae interjected, "does he really know how to operate a rocket?"

Fawhikwuff smiled. "Hesdihe is my best friend. Really, he's my only friend. And yes, he really can operate a rocket."

Annie Mae and Chloe exchanged a look Fawhikwuff didn't like.

"What?"

"Isn't it obvious?" Chloe asked. "If Hesdihe can fly a rocket, you need to call him here and let him in. Have him possess Buzz or the other one and then we all can see when you win!"

"That sounds like way more work than it's worth."

"Think of it as a backup plan. What if something happens?" Annie Mae asked.

Fawhikwuff smiled. He liked the thought of a backup plan. And of seeing Hesdihe, perhaps for the last time. "All right, you two, you win. I'll go call him." He pulled out his demon phone and stepped into the hallway, leaving the two girls alone in the room as he hit the call button for his best friend.

It rang once, twice, then it was picked up by a shouting voice. Fawhikwuff moved the phone away from his ear until the noise died down,

"Hesdihe?" Fawhikwuff called into the phone.

"Did you get that?" Hesdihe's voice crackled in his ear finally.

"No. Did I get what? What is going on?"

"You're probably picking up the Fartlands in the background. A lot of smelly toots today," Hesdihe said. "The tooters are going crazy. They actually think you're going to make it to the moon, and the tooters aren't a fan of a demon taking control of the moon. Get this: They actually think that if demons have control of the moon, it's only a matter of time before the demons take over the whole human world, and they really hate that thought."

"Are the tooters coming here to stop me then? Hesdihe, should I be worried? Should we buy hazmat suits?"

The tooters were small, about the size of your average garden gnome, and if it wasn't for their lethal toots, they would be easy to defeat. The gas they produced made demons feel woozy, though, while their little poop clouds could put humans in a coma or even kill them.

Fawhikwuff looked back at the closed door. Behind it stood Annie Mae and Chloe, two humans he never wanted to have to meet a tooter. Well, at least not Annie Mae. If Chloe met one, he wouldn't cry.

"No," Hesdihe's voice snapped him back into focus. "The tooters won't leave the Fartlands. They're just freaking out because—they're just freaking out. For no good reason, ha-ha. Dang tooters."

"That was really convincing, Hesdihe. Why are you even in the Fartlands?"

"Can't I just visit the tooters?"

"You hate the tooters. Everyone hates the tooters. You say they are a smelly waste of sociality and the only reason you'd ever want to be a human would be so you wouldn't know they existed."

"Well, the fastest way to you is through the Fartlands."

"The fastest way to *me*? You're coming here? Why are you coming here?"

"Wow. Really feeling the love."

"Sorry, but you know what I mean. Why are you coming here?"

"Perlicudak was spotted in the Fartlands. That's actually probably the bigger reason why the tooters are freaking out, if I'm being completely honest. They think you must be close to winning this contest if he's taking the long way to the human world, the route through here, where he should be able to go undetected. The tooters are panicking. They think he wouldn't bother unless there is a real chance of you conquering the moon, which again, they don't want to see happen."

Fawhikwuff ran a hand over Michael Collins' face and let out a heavy sigh. "Well, he can't hurt Annie Mae. He knows that. He's not stupid."

"No, but he could do something to you still, or to the rocket. That's why I'm coming. I figured you could use another demon by your side."

"And when were you going to tell me this?"

"I was planning to call after I escaped the Fartlands, but this is better. Look, I should be there by tomorrow, in plenty of time before the launch. Just watch your back and be careful. I don't know what Perlicudak is planning, but I'm sure it's not good."

"Will do. Thank you, Hesdihe. See you tomorrow." Fawhikwuff hung up. It looked like the girls were going to get what they wanted. He had no choice.

He returned to the room to rejoin the girls. But he froze the moment he opened the door.

"How nice of you to join us!" Perlicudak cooed at him. He held Chloe's struggling form in a death grip.

"Let her go," Fawhikwuff ordered.

"You know, I never saw you as a Michael, Fawhikwuff." Perlicudak smiled.

Annie Mae ran over and hid behind Fawhikwuff.

"They can't all be your children. I think this one will be mine. If you want her back, you'll meet me here, in your demon form, at nine the morning of the launch. Or perhaps I'll just get a tasty brat snack." Perlicudak made a biting sound and, still holding Chloe, vanished in a cloud of smoke, taking her with him.

"NO!"

76

08 DAYS, 11 HOURS, 41 MINUTES, 16 SECONDS, AND COUNTING TO CONQUER A PLANET

With a mighty blow, Fawhikwuff slammed Michael Collins' fist into the wall, denting it. He let out a scream of frustration. Quickly, Annie Mae shushed him. Fawhikwuff obliged, slinking into the closest chair.

"I put her in danger. I put you both in danger. All I ever do is screw up you humans' lives. This is why demons and humans aren't ever friends."

"Do you really think things would be better if you were human?"

"I don't know, but I think Chloe wouldn't be kidnapped by a demon if I were human."

Annie Mae nodded her head and the two sat in silence for a moment. "So, what do we do now?"

"Now? Now I wait until I can meet Perlicudak here and save Chloe. I'll send Hesdihe home when he gets here. It's too late. That's that. I'm going to go to Hell."

"No!"

"You can go stay with Hesdihe in the demon realm until this

is all done. I can't be on the rocket and also ensure your safety —and save Chloe."

"But you will lose. Do we have to save Chloe? She's still a bully."

Fawhikwuff looked at Annie Mae in surprise. "Perlicudak wasn't kidding when he said he would eat her. She may not be the world's nicest person, but our rule has always been 'no killing'. I don't like her, but you don't really want her dead, do you?"

"No, of course not. I just. I don't want to lose you."

"I know. I don't want to lose you, either." Fawhikwuff knew there was no way for him to save Chloe and go to the moon. But he didn't really have a choice, did he? Chloe wouldn't have been taken by a demon if it wasn't for his stupid bet. He would have been fine to go to the moon if he hadn't been sloppy and gotten on the government's watch list. He had screwed up so many times, but he wasn't about to be selfish enough to let a young girl die because of him.

"Chloe shouldn't pay the price just because I am an idiot," he said, putting his thoughts into words, stressing it to himself as much as to Annie Mae.

"No. But you shouldn't go to Hell, either."

77

04 DAYS, 16 HOURS, 00 MINUTES, 16 SECONDS, AND COUNTING TO CONQUER A PLANET

The morning of the next demon day, Fawhikwuff left Michael Collins at ten minutes before eight o'clock to wait in the designated room. It had a view of the launch pad, where, at any moment, the rocket to the moon would take off without him. He would stay on Earth.

Perlicudak showed up right at nine, a smug look on his face and a squirming Chloe locked under one of his arms. "Good. You came," Perlicudak hissed.

"You win, Perlicudak. Give her back," Fawhikwuff insisted.

"Where is Annie Mae?" Perlicudak asked.

"I didn't realize you cared about her."

Perlicudak gave a laugh. "Trust me, I don't. I just want to make sure you're not tricking me here."

Fawhikwuff nodded. "She's with Lolli. I wasn't going to let you be anywhere near her."

"Well, let's watch the launch together, shall we? This is a big deal for the dumb humans. Then I will give you back your Chloe."

An overhead speaker crackled to life. A voice came over it: "TEN!" The countdown had begun for Apollo 11's takeoff.

"It's over, Perlicudak! Give her back! You win!" Fawhikwuff had to shout to be heard over the rocket revving up outside, building toward takeoff.

"When it hits zero!" Perlicudak yelled back.

"Fawhikwuff, go!" Chloe yelled next. "Get on the rocket! I know what happens if you lose! I'm so sorry! Tell Annie Mae I'm sorry! Just go!"

"I'm not leaving you," Fawhikwuff promised.

"SEVEN!"

"I want you to!" Chloe screamed. "You shouldn't go to Hell because of me!"

"And you shouldn't die because of me!"

"Oh, for cute," Perlicudak mocked and then made a gagging noise. "I mean, oh, for barf!"

"FIVE!"

"Just go!" Chloe yelled.

Fawhikwuff shook his head. He couldn't leave a child to die for him.

"YOU IDIOT!" Chloe thrashed in Perlicudak's grip.

"I think everyone would agree with you on that one, Chloe! I sure do!" Perlicudak commented.

"ONE!"

With a tremendous roar and quake that reverberated into the Earth and shook the entire building, Apollo 11 lifted. It left its home planet.

Perlicudak released Chloe then. A deal was a deal. She quickly ran to Fawhikwuff. Although she was still calling him an idiot, her embrace said something else.

"I will see you in Hell," Perlicudak grinned.

"That'll have to be after I watch you do the chicken dance," Fawhikwuff taunted with a knowing grin.

"What are you talking about?"

"You just lost."

"No, he didn't." Chloe looked up at Fawhikwuff, her

eyebrows squeezed together in confusion. "Apollo 11 just took off, Fawhikwuff. Right there. If you crane your neck a little, you can still see it. See? Right. There. You lost."

"Except the Michael Collins onboard isn't actually Michael Collins." Fawhikwuff turned from Chloe to Perlicudak. "It's Hesdihe, my buddy, my pal. And he knows rockets better than any other demon. His skillset is very undervalued at the nightmare division. He is aboard Apollo 11, and when they reach the moon, he will claim it in my name, and I will win the bet. And Perlicudak? You. Will. Lose."

"No."

"Oh, yes. I suggest you go home and prepare your chicken dance, because you are about to be a loser. And don't bother attacking us. I knew you'd be mad, so I summoned members of the council here to oversee that these last few days don't end in chaos that could risk exposing us even more to the human world. After all, we don't want a simple bet to turn into a violent game, now do we?"

A cloaked figure entered the room, from behind Fawhikwuff. "It's time for all of us to go back to Demon Land, Perlicudak," said the High Council member. "Your only hope now is that the humans failed at building that rocket and Hesdihe can't fix their terrible errors. Otherwise, I'm afraid Fawhikwuff is right. You have lost a bet for the first time."

78

03 DAYS, 15 HOURS, 21 MINUTES, 32 SECONDS, AND COUNTING TO CONQUER A PLANET

Lolli punched Fawhikwuff in the arm. "You better figure out a way to summon me so I can hang out with you guys still."

Lolli, Fawhikwuff, the council member, and Annie Mae stood just at the edge of town, saying their goodbyes. It was time for Fawhikwuff to take Annie Mae back to his home, which would become their home.

"We will," Fawhikwuff promised, "otherwise me and Annie Mae are just a summon away." Fawhikwuff gave the girl a hug. As soon as he released her, she went and hugged Annie Mae.

"Bye," Annie Mae said softly.

"We'll be back soon, I promise," Fawhikwuff said, but that didn't make saying goodbye any easier.

"There's someone else who wanted to say goodbye." Lolli pulled away from Annie Mae, a smile on her face.

"Who?" Fawhikwuff asked as Finn, the boy from Annie Mae's class, stepped into the clearing, a smile on his face, and a droopy daisy in his hand. "Oh. Gross."

79

02 DAYS, 02 HOURS, 13 MINUTES, 46 SECONDS, AND COUNTING TO CONQUER A PLANET

Tomorrow they would enter the Fartlands, but tonight, their last night in the human world for a while, found Fawhikwuff and Annie Mae on their backs, on a rooftop owned by someone they didn't know, looking up at the stars and watching the night slip away.

"Are there going to be stars?" Annie Mae asked.

"In the demon world? Yeah, there are all kinds of stars. More than you can see here. We'll have to get a new place when you move in. I'll make sure it has a roof like this so we can watch the stars whenever you want."

Annie Mae smiled wide. "Thank you, Fawhikwuff."

"For what? Ruining your life?"

"Saving it."

Fawhikwuff smiled. "I didn't save it; you did." Fawhikwuff reached into his pocket and pulled out a package of coconut scout cookies. He tore the paper wrapping apart and placed them between them before he took one and ate it.

"You got a box?"

"We sold so many boxes of this crap, I think we've earned it."

"Is it stolen?"

"Borrowed," Fawhikwuff said. "Just eat a cookie, Annie Mae."

Hesitantly, Annie Mae did as Fawhikwuff requested. "They actually are pretty good."

"The High Council member will get here tomorrow with Perlicudak so we can all cross together. For now, just enjoy the stars. And the cookies."

PART V

WILL THE MOON BE MINE?

80

A NEW NORMAL

And so, Annie Mae and Fawhikwuff returned to the demon realm accompanied by Perlicudak and the member of the High Council.

For a long few days, as Apollo 11 made its way to the moon, Annie Mae and Fawhikwuff spent their time fixing up Fawhikwuff's awful apartment so it could accommodate both of them while they searched for a new home.

They got Annie Mae registered for school, too. They even met a few of her future classmates who all thought it was totally amazing that she was human.

A demon came to the house one afternoon and told them he worked for the department that made some humans have dyslexia and social issues. He fessed up that he was the one responsible for Annie Mae's struggles with those issues. The demon offered to "fix" her, since she was now Fawhikwuff's daughter. Fawhikwuff and Annie Mae swiftly sent the demon away. Annie Mae liked who she was. Neither she nor Fawhikwuff would change her. She didn't need to be "fixed".

81

00 DAYS, 03 HOURS, 26 MINUTES, 17 SECONDS, AND COUNTING TO CONQUER A PLANET

The demon pub was packed to watch Apollo 11 set down on the moon. They were eager to see if Fawhikwuff would truly win.

In a booth across from Annie Mae, Fawhikwuff refused mugs of Tears of Blind Rage from demons who slapped him on the back anyway and told him how happy they were for him. He wasn't making that mistake again.

All eyes were on the television behind the bar. It didn't normally play human channels, but the bar was packed at the prospect of seeing Perlicudak do the chicken dance. Everyone was eager to monitor what was happening.

A number on the screen beneath "Time to Lunar Landing" was counting down. The end of the bet was getting closer, too, as human voices on the TV commented on and discussed the historic moment.

Everyone held their breath, watching and waiting. At about five minutes to landing, the footage changed to crowds taking it all in. People all over the world were following the event, too, the commentator remarked. Little did he know it wasn't just his world.

When the craft finally landed on the moon, the pub erupted in cheers, almost drowning out the voice of astronaut Neil Armstrong, who could be heard saying, "Houston, Tranquility Base here. The Eagle has landed."

It wasn't over yet, though. Demons and humans alike watched anxiously for the astronauts to emerge, Hesdihe among them, and to step onto the moon. Would it really be claimed as Fawhikwuff's? Could Hesdihe pull it off?

The first astronaut emerged.

"Who is that? That Hesdihe?" A demon shouted and was instantly shushed.

"That's one small step for man," the astronaut said, his boots hitting the surface of the moon, stirring up a small dust cloud. "One giant leap for—"

"Fawhikwuff!" A second astronaut shouted, also jumping from the module, landing awkwardly and directly on top of the first astronaut, causing him to topple, even if in seeming slow motion, to the moon's surface. The demons knew it was Hesdihe. The humans must have assumed Michael Collins had just lost his marbles.

Hesdihe, as Michael Collins, turned toward the camera then and announced, "I declare the moon the property of the demon Fawhikwuff."

Screens everywhere immediately went blank.

"I'm sorry, ladies and gentlemen, we'll be back in just a moment," a news anchor said, and the black screen cut away to a commercial featuring a little animated flying man on the moon who had been freed by the energy that Quisp Cereal gave him.

"I won," Fawhikwuff said softly to himself before looking around at all the faces in the pub, every one of them beaming in his direction. "I won!" he yelled a little louder and everyone cheered. "I actually won!"

Instead of cheering, Perlicudak scowled.

"Chicken dance!" Annie Mae yelled, pointing across the bar toward Perlicudak. The whole pub began to chant with her: "Chick! En! Dance!" "Chick! En! Dance!"

Perlicudak stood and looked around, recognizing that everyone there had wanted him to fail and were now cheering that he had. It's tough realizing "supporters" and "friends" were only supporters and friends because you were on top. Every lung in the place called for Perlicudak's humiliation. He had no choice but to go through with it. The greatest demon ever had lost the silliest bet ever.

Perlicudak rose to his feet. He extended all of his arms. "I don't want to be a chicken," he said, flapping his elbows.

"Louder!" Fawhikwuff yelled.

"Sing!" Annie Mae cheered.

"I don't want to be a duck." Perlicudak was singing now, his movements in line with the song. "So, kiss my butt. Cluck, cluck, cluck, cluck. I don't want to be a chicken, I don't want to be a duck, so kiss my butt." Perlicudak even shook his butt as he sang. "Cluck, cluck, cluck, cluck."

"Come on," Fawhikwuff said to Annie Mae, and the two of them got up, joining the dance. Soon every demon in the bar was shaking their butts and singing along. Even Perlicudak started having fun. "I don't want to be a chicken, I don't want to be a duck, so kiss my butt!"

ACKNOWLEDGMENTS

Up until others actually got to read this story, people often thought I was pulling their leg when I said I was writing about a cookie-selling demon who wanted to take over the moon in 1969. I am so excited that I got to share this story. Thank you, Reader, for coming on this journey and hearing Fawhikwuff's and Annie Mae's tale! I wrote this book because I needed a fun, light-hearted tale full of goofy wild energy that I hope made you smile.

Like any book, this one took a village, and I am beyond grateful for my village.

Thank you especially to my wonderfully supportive family, especially Mom, Dad, Reggie, and Claire. I love you guys. Thank you for always having my back, being my beta readers and test audience, helping with edits, and letting me ramble on about my stories always. You guys are amazing!

Huge thank you to Anna, my editor at Bow's Bookshelf for embracing, loving, and supporting this strange story and for taking a chance on publishing it. She has been such a wonderful light in this book's journey and I can no longer imagine Demon Scout without her being a part of it.

Thank you to all my wonderful friends who have been there for me, including my Morbid Expert Jeremiah W. Larson, my Law Expert Autumn Zierman, my Child Psychology Expert Emma Haugen, my Sorority Big Cheyenne Valstar and her adorable dog Nova, my Theater Child Phoenix Ocean, Abby Longnaker, Naomi Desai, Jessie Wu, Diana Tran, K Johnson,

Asher Noriega, Hannah Power, Lucy Nicodemus, and so, so, so many others! I am so blessed to have you all in my life.

Thank you to all of my amazing sorority sisters of Theta Phi Alpha!

Thank you to Marcia and Brian Freeman for all your advice and support, and thank you to Marcia Freeman and Tony Dierckins for helping me look over contracts and pointing me in the right directions.

Thank you to Lapshan Fong, Adrian Shirk, Laura Diamond, and all the amazing and supportive faculty at Pratt Institute. Thank you to all the other teachers, too, who helped shape me at St. James, Denfeld High School, and Pratt.

Thank you to everyone who agreed to beta read anything for me, everyone who has given me advice in-studio, and everyone who has helped guide and shape my work. Writing only gets better with feedback. You all prove that again and again.

Thank you to my high school English teacher Mrs. Mickle, who, on graduation night, backstage, before I got my diploma, gave me a hug and told me she had read my first script and urged me to look more seriously into writing. Thank you for helping to spark that first step, both in your words and by having me write that script for class.

Last, but in no way least, thank you to all writers also suffering from dyslexia, POTS, auditory memory dysfunction, gastroparesis, anxiety, and/or migraines who also came on this journey.

ABOUT THE AUTHOR

Charleigh Frederick is an author, playwright, and screenwriter from Duluth, Minnesota, whose works blur the line between good and evil. She is an undergraduate at Pratt Institute in Brooklyn, New York, pursuing a bachelor's degree in Writing. Charleigh also enjoys weaving baskets, obsessing over whatever she is currently reading, and spending time with family and friends. For more on Charleigh and her work, visit https://charleighfrederick.wixsite.com/cswrite

CAN'T WAIT TO READ MORE?

Join our Bow's Bookshelf Reader's Club for new projects, deals, and giveaways. Sign up at Bowsbookshelf.com or follow us on social media!